BRIDGER TRAIL

ALSO BY B.N. RUNDELL

Rindin' Lonesome

Star Dancer

The Christmas Bear

Buckskin Chronicles

McCain Chronicles

Plainsman Western Series

Rocky Mountain Saint Series

Stonecroft Saga

BRIDGER TRAIL

McCain Cronicles
Book Eight

B.N. Rundell

WOLFPACK
PUBLISHING
— EST 2013 —

Bridger Trail
Paperback Edition
Copyright © 2024 B.N. Rundell

Wolfpack Publishing
701 S. Howard Ave. 106-324
Tampa, Florida 33609

wolfpackpublishing.com

Paperback ISBN 978-1-63977-372-5
eBook ISBN 978-1-63977-371-8
LCCN 2024931906

To my Lord and Savior, Jesus. Thank you for giving me a reprieve and the time to finish this book. May it bring glory to you and may others come to know you.

BRIDGER TRAIL

CHAPTER 1

WAGONS

He sat tall in the saddle, broad shouldered, dark blonde hair that tickled his collar, clean shaven and by most standards, at least when established by the fairer sex, he was a handsome man. With canvas britches, linen shirt, leather vest, and a flat brimmed black felt hat, he caught the eye of the ladies, the envy of the men, and the respect of all who knew him. Elijah McCain had led a company of Union cavalry in the late war, fighting at Shenandoah and Appomattox Court House with General Phil Sheridan and mustered out at the rank of Lieutenant Colonel. But the last letter from the home of his wife's family, begged him to come home as she was failing and might not last out the year.

It was at her bedside that he learned of their twin sons, who had joined the Union army, but deserted and went west to seek their fortune in the newly discovered gold fields. Her last whispered request was, "Bring them home, Eli, there's a home here for them, they could take over the farm and make a good life for themselves. Please, bring them home?" It was while he was at his wife's family farm that he outfitted himself for what promised to be a long journey and search for his step-sons, twins Jubal and Joshua. Eli had married their mother when she was in the family way by her husband, a classmate of his from West Point who died at their first duty station, Jefferson Barracks, having elicited a promise from Eli to take care of his wife. And Eli did just that, he married the wife of Ferdinand Paine, Margaret, and made a life for her and her sons. But the army kept him away from home for most of their married lives, yet he developed a special fondness for Margaret and did his best by her and the boys.

He outfitted himself at the farm where they were known to breed some of the best horses around. He chose a claybank, or line-back red dun, stallion, a cross breed Tennessee Walker and Morgan, for his mount. He had a local saddle maker build him a custom saddle, similar to the Mexican Charro saddle with a flat-topped saddle horn and high cantle with swells on the pommel, but resembled the Moorish saddles with round skirts and center fire rigged, with custom saddlebags and scabbards for his two rifles he preferred, a Spencer .52 caliber and a Winchester Yellow Boy .44. He had kept a mustang gelding he used while stationed at Fort Laramie, and now put the dapple grey to work as his packhorse. The two horses had become inseparable companions and the grey often followed free-rein without the need for a lead rope.

Eli had become accustomed to always having his Bowie knife in a sheath at his back that hung between his shoulders, a LeMat pistol in a custom made holster that hung under his belt in the small of his back, and a butt-forward mounted holster on his left hip to give access to his new Remington Army metallic cartridge conversion .44 pistol. Aboard the pack horse rode his Colt Revolving shotgun, a handy weapon in close-order fighting.

When he set out on his search to fulfill the promise made to his wife, he had no idea the quest would take him over a year and across most of the western wilderness of this growing nation, but after covering most of the gold fields, going into the early settlements of the northwest, and following the trail of his shanghaied sons down to the San Francisco bay and beyond, he finally found them and convinced them to join him on a trail drive to take a herd of a thousand cavalry remounts back east to Fort Hays, Kansas that would provide a nest egg for his two lovesick sons that were determined to get married to a pair of beautiful sisters and settle down on the family farm and raise horses.

Once the horses were delivered, Eli found himself a bit footloose and uncertain about his immediate future, but a request from his old cavalry commander, General Phil Sheridan, to join him in the early stages of his winter campaign to put a stop to the continual raiding of the Cheyenne Dog Soldiers and their Arapaho allies, prompted him to return to Fort Hays and become a scout for the cavalry. But that had proven to be something he no longer had a willingness to do and together with his friend who had joined him on the trail drive, Charlie Two Toes, he joined up with a wagon train of settlers and would-be gold miners bound for the Montana gold fields. After the people of the train asked them to guide them the rest of the way, they agreed, but the hard winter had forced them to spend time at Fort Laramie before departing to the north.

The usual route, the Bozeman Trail, had been closed by the army and the signing of the Fort Laramie Treaty of

1868 between the army and the Sioux nations under the leadership of Red Cloud. Now, Eli was readying himself and the wagon train to begin the almost five hundred mile trek to Montana via the Bridger Trail, the lesser used route also discovered by Jim Bridger and now provided the shortest route for the gold-hungry settlers that had fled the war-torn east in hopes of a new beginning in the west.

He sat with a glassy-eyed stare as he looked at the low flames of his campfire. He had spent the winter in the lodge with Bald Eagle, *Neiwoo*, or Grandma, a widow woman of the Arapaho. He kept her supplied with meat and other staples, she did the cooking and they both had a good winter. He moved his camp to the edge of the trees on the northeast of the big meadow outside Fort Laramie where the wagons had spent the winter, all but Charlie Two Toes and his new wife who commandeered one of the two cabins in the trees. He was just a short walk from the cabins, and he was thinking about the coming journey. As was typical of the wanderers of the time, Eli had taken every opportunity to glean as much information about the Bridger Trail from the troops, scouts, and leftover mountain men that had been over the trail and now had his mental map of the entire trek, but there was always something missing or changed by the time they traveled over that country.

A hail from the trees came from a familiar voice and Charlie Two Toes and two other men came into the ring of light, the golden glow of the fire illuminating their faces to show Charlie and two strangers. Charlie called out, "Mind if we come in? Got some fellas wantin' to talk."

"Come ahead on! Coffee's hot," answered Eli, reaching for the pot to warm up his own cupful.

Charlie stepped closer, motioned to the two men following, "This hyar's George Catlin, he's fixin' to set up a gen'l store in Virginia City, Montana. He's got some wagons he wants to come with us on the train."

Eli frowned, glanced to Charlie at the mention of "us." There had been no discussion of him coming on the trail since he was a newlywed, and they were already expecting their firstborn just anytime soon. Eli had assumed they would be staying in the cabin near the fort, at least for the time being. He had been told by Charlie's wife's brother that Meaghan was well set financially, and he had assumed they would find themselves a home in a more civilized part of the country, like a city or something. Even though Charlie was Pawnee and not accustomed to the settled life in the city, Eli thought he could become accustomed to the comfortable life. He chuckled as he looked to the newcomers, extended his hand to shake with Catlin as he turned to introduce the third man, "And this is my ramrod, Dre Jackson."

Eli extended his hand to the ramrod, and nodded, "And I'm Elijah, Eli, McCain." He paused, took a sip of coffee, motioned to the others to help themselves, and asked, "How many wagons?"

"Five, solid, well-built, each with a four-up of good stout mules, and we have an extra team as well."

"What're you haulin'?" asked Eli, there was something about the beady-eyed man that just did not sit right with him. His eyes were always dancing around under those bushy, black eyebrows as if looking for something to steal, or fearful of being discovered. There was nothing imposing nor intimidating about the man, he just appeared to be nervous.

"Everything we need for a complete general store.

Dry goods, foodstuffs, canned goods, guns, ammo, mining supplies, you name it, we'll be carryin' it."

"How many men?"

"Two per wagon."

"Will they fight?"

Catlin frowned, leaned back, "Whaddaya mean, fight?"

"If we are hit by natives, renegades."

Catlin seemed to relax at Eli's description, nodded, "I'm sure they will. I didn't hire 'em to fight, but they all wanna get to the gold fields. I'm stakin' 'em for their drivin'."

Eli glanced to Charlie, read nothing in his expression and looked back to Catlin, "We have thirty other wagons, families all. You'll have ten unattached men, you'll keep them away from the womenfolk, understand?"

"I understand. But these men aren't looking for women, they're looking for gold."

"If they wear pants, they're always lookin' for women, and I'll have no problems, understand?"

"I do. I just want to get my goods to the goldfields and get my business set up. We'll all do our share, yessir."

"We're leavin' at first light, and I don't mean sunup, first light."

"Yessir," replied Catlin, nodding as he stood and tossed aside the dregs of his coffee. He disappeared into the night as Eli looked at Charlie and cocked one eyebrow up as he grinned at his friend, "Us?"

"Wal, I figgered you'd just get lost without me, so..." he shrugged, grinning.

"What about Meaghan?"

"Wal, seein' as how she's in a family way, she thought

it'd be best to go with her brother an' sister-in-law, have a woman by her side for the big event. You know."

"I kinda thought she might like for both of you to come."

"We talked about it, but them wagons ride kinda rough, an' this is her first time, so..." He let the thought dangle as his eyes glazed over while he looked into the flames of the fire, a practice he seldom did, always preserving his night vision for whatever might come. But somber thoughts of reflection and wonder often overcame any man that sat beside a campfire.

CHAPTER 2

EMBARK

Eli sat with one elbow on the pommel, leaning forward, as he watched the wagons begin to stretch out. The people had drawn lots to determine their position in the line and LaVern Hackworth had drawn the first in line and he was grinning broadly as he nodded to Eli and stretched his four-up of mules to take the lead. Thirty-four wagons followed, with the five wagons of Catlin bringing up the rear. Each day the wagons would rotate, with the lead wagon going to the rear and each wagon moving up the line. Eli had made a walk around the day before, checking with each family and the condition of their wagons and teams. Most had the Studebaker wagon made in South Bend, Indiana in the factory of the Studebaker brothers on the line of what was known as Prairie Schooners. Eli was surprised the trader Catlin also had prairie schooners rather than the heavier Sante Fe style wagon that could carry over three ton of goods, but with each wagon having a four-up hitch of mules, he supposed those wagons would carry a sufficient load for the trader's mercantile store.

The wagons groaned to the same tune as they rocked from their ruts made deeper by the wagons sitting through the winter without moving, and the trace chains sang the high-pitched tones of sopranos in the choir, and the groan of cold wood and axles provided the bass section of the wagon chorus. Horses and mules leaned into their collars, dug hooves deep in the grassy flat, and rocked the wagons to start. Drivers shouted, cracked whips, slapped reins and pleaded encouragement for the animals to do their best. Eli knew it would be several days on the trail before the animals would accept the routine that took them from the greening grasses of the meadow that had been their home for the winter. But the warm sun rising off their right shoulders warmed the backs of the animals and drivers alike and the train began to stretch out in a long line of rocking white canopies. It would soon become the rhythmic accompaniment for the journey and one that would impress itself on the minds and hearts of all who traveled.

When the trader's wagons neared, Eli nudged Rusty alongside the last of the family's wagons driven by Max McCoy with his wife Violet. They were a young couple and one of the few families without children, but it would not long be the case, as Violet was blooming with anticipation as she rested her hands on the top of her growing middle. Max looked at Eli and asked, "Bout how far you reckon we'll make each day?"

"Oh, dependin' on the weather and the condition of the trail, anywhere from fifteen to twenty or so miles. 'Course we'll hafta stop mid-day and give the animals a bit of a rest, water, and such, but we'll make good time."

"How far to Virginia City?"

"Little over five hundred miles."

Max frowned, obviously thinking, then grinned, "So, a little more'n thirty days?"

"At least that. There will be times we hafta layover for a day or two for repairs, either to the wagons or the road, and there's always the weather that likes to interfere."

Max nodded, glanced to his wife who was holding tightly to his arm and smiling up at him, "We'll be fine, sweetheart, honest," she assured him.

Eli chuckled, knowing she had no more control on the time than he did with the wagons, but such was the way of things and there would be more than their share of challenges before this journey was over.

Most of the wagons were drawn by a team of horses or mules, a few had a double hitch with four animals, and those with two usually had good, sturdy draft horses, and a few had the big draft breeds like Percheron. The people had spent their spare time during the winter repairing the wagons and harness and most were in good condition for the journey, but there were always things that could break, or wear out, although Eli was pleased to learn that among the families, there was a good blacksmith who hoped to open a shop in the gold fields and could fix just about anything on a wagon or harness.

Charlie Two Toes had left early for his scout of the trail and Eli had utmost confidence in his friend, knowing he would do his best to keep them out of trouble, and his best was far better than most. As Eli watched the wagons pass, he stood in his stirrups and looked to the back of the train, seeing the trader's wagons coming into line and stretching out. There was still something about that trader that made Eli a tad uncomfortable, and he did not like that feeling that seemed to crawl up his spine and linger at the back of his neck, making his hair stand on end. That had always been a sign of trouble and it was too early for this train to already have trouble, for that would come soon enough and there was no need to hurry it along. He nudged Rusty around and started back to the tail of the line, wanting to give the wagons of the trader one last look-see.

Eli was surprised to see the first wagon was driven by Catlin himself, with one of the roustabouts riding on the seat beside him, the four-up of bay mules leaning into their collars. Eli moved alongside the lead wagon and looked up at Catlin, "When we make camp each night, we'll be posting guards and every man will take his turn, that includes your men."

"Of course, of course. Wouldn't expect anything different, Mr. McCain."

"Eli will do. Everything alright—no problems with your wagons or anything?"

"Everything's fine and dandy, Eli, thank you."

"Good, good. I'll drop back and meet the rest of your men," added Eli, reining up on the big claybank. He pulled aside, let the wagon pass and moved beside the second wagon. Driven by the man introduced as Catlin's ramrod, Dre Jackson. He was a swarthy colored man who sat wide legged with his heels on the footrest and seemingly crowding out his roustabout, also a colored man. Eli spoke to the driver, "I told Catlin that when we camp, we'll be posting guards every night and you men will have a turn at it as will all the others."

"That'd be fine, Colonel, yessir."

Eli frowned at the man's use of the military rank and twisted in his saddle to look up at the man, "Do I know you?"

"We met th'other night, Colonel, 'member?"

"No, I mean other than that."

"Yessir, we met at a little dust-up on Arikaree Creek. You an' some other fellas were on a bit of an island in the crick and me'n muh fellow so'jers come along to hep you out a mite." He grinned as he looked at Eli, remembering the time the band of scouts had been overrun by about a thousand Cheyenne and Arapaho led by Roman Nose. "And 'fore that, we he'ped you out at the Saline River when some o' them Dog So'jers were tryin' to get yo' hosses."

Eli grinned, remembering, shook his head and said, "Company F, 10th Cavalry!"

"Yassuh," chuckled the big muleskinner, slapping reins to the rumps of the big mules.

"Any others of your outfit come along?"

"Yassuh. We heard 'bout you'n Charlie leavin' after that Washita River massacre, an' after what we'd been seein', several of us thought we might like to try diggin' for gold instead o' killin' Injuns. So, when Mr. Catlin came 'round lookin' for some drivers an' such, he said he'd grubstake us in the gold fields, so..." he shrugged, grinning.

"Well, I'm glad to have you with us, Jackson. I'm hopin' we won't be needin' to do any fighting of the natives, but you never can tell. Ol' Red Cloud signed the treaty, but the government hasta ratify it and the soldiers hafta enforce it, and in most cases there's just too many 'haftas' connected with the treaties to keep them in force by either side."

"I unnerstan' Colonel, more's the pity too. With all this land, you'd think there'd be room fo' eve'body, but..." he shrugged, shaking his head at the futility of it all.

"Well, at least this is not a long trip. We should make it in five or six weeks, dependin'."

"Dependin'?"

"You know, the weather, the natives, the wagons, there's as many variables as there are people on the train."

Eli dropped back and talked with the rest of the drivers and roustabouts, passing along the word about needing to take their turn at standing guard. He was pleased to meet the other men of the 10th, confident they would be an asset in any conflict, but the other men, drivers and roustabouts, looked a mite scruffy and might not be as dependable. But there was nothing to be done about it now and Eli rode back along the train, making his way to the lead of the wagons.

He planned to make a stop at a point known as Register Rock, he wanted those new to the use of rifles to get in a little practice and he would use the men of the 10th to give some instruction.

CHAPTER 3

REGISTER ROCK

The pale grey cliffs hung like a long curtain from the broad shoulders of the wide flat mesa that stood sentinel over the meandering North Platte River. Etched into the sandstone cliffs were the mementos of multitudes of travelers that had stopped beneath the long shadows and sought to memorialize their passage by carving names and dates into the soft stone. Eli had required the families and others to arm every person that would be capable of using a firearm to defend the families of the wagon train against any attackers, native, renegade, outlaws and highwaymen. But many of those same travelers had never had any instruction in the use of the rifles or pistols and without some direction, would probably be more dangerous than helpful.

As the wagons neared the long buff-colored wall that stood apart from the riverbed, Eli saw Charlie standing beside his buckskin, watching the approach of the wagon train. Eli reined up beside him and stepped down, grinning at his friend, "You ready to try to teach some pilgrims how to shoot?"

Charlie grinned, shook his head, "I have found that there are some that can shoot, some that can be taught to shoot, and some that should never get near any kind of weapon!"

"Well, we gotta try. There's three former soldiers from the 10th Cavalry that I thought we'd get to help out. I'll go get 'em; you can start settin' up somethin' for 'em to shoot at."

At Charlie's nod, Eli stepped back aboard Rusty and reined him around to ride along the wagons and go fetch the men from the 10th to get things started. It was late morning and they needed time for a nooning, but they also needed to spend as much time on the trail to make progress their first day out. The freighters were at the riverbank, watering their stock and checking their gear when Eli approached.

"Yo, Felix!" he greeted the former sergeant, and stepped down, drew near the husky man who was grinning broadly, and responded, "Howdy Colonel. What're we fixin' to do here?"

Eli chuckled. "We've got a bunch of pilgrims that don't know much of anything about what a rifle is for and what end the bullet comes out, so, I thought we'd stop here a spell, let you and your men give 'em a little instruction on the best way to keep from gettin' kilt if'n we get attacked by some renegade Sioux."

"I thought ol' Red Cloud signed a treaty to behave himself," replied Felix, frowning.

"He did, but what most folks don't understand about natives is that one man cannot speak for another, and just because Red Cloud signed, does not mean any of the other bands will hold to the treaty nor will the young bucks that are lookin' to gain honors and steal horses and such."

"Sounds like we're gonna need ever' rifle we got!"

"Only if they can hit what they shoot at!" added Eli, chuckling and shaking his head. "I'll ride through the wagons, get everybody over yonder near the cliffs. Charlie's settin' up some targets, and you and your men can help us get 'em lined out and hopefully not kill anybody."

Felix shook his head, sighed heavily and motioned to his fellow former soldiers and brought them closer to fill them in on what was planned.

Charlie had gathered an assortment of chunks of wood, branches, cast-offs from wagons, parts of whiskey barrels, broken wheel hubs, anything that would absorb a bullet without causing a ricochet and hurting someone. He lined them out against the sandstone cliffs, knowing the soft sandstone would take the bullets without any ricochets. Eli rode alongside the lined out wagons, telling the people about the time of target practice and firmly admonished the people of the necessity of the practice. "It might make the difference between surviving the journey or being buried alongside the trail."

That got their attention and all the newbies at shooting were soon lined out before the targets, rifles and pistols at their sides and awaiting the instructors. The long curtain of cliffs stretched a half-mile from the southwest to the northeast, standing off from the river about three hundred yards with the wagons lined out behind the shooters. Felix stepped before the people, holding his Sharps rifle with the long telescopic sight attached, across his chest. "Folks, me'n muh frien's here have been asked to show you a bit about shootin'. We spent a few years in the Union army and afterwards with the 10th Cavalry fightin' Injuns, so we done our share. We ain't no experts, but we knows whut we doin' an' we'll do our best to help you. Now, I'm gonna show you what a rifle can do, and what you might need to learn."

He turned to face the cliffs, spotted a chunk of a stump, hollered to Charlie, "Could'ja put a white rock, 'bout the size o' yo' fist, atop that stump?"

Charlie nodded, looked about for a rock, placed it on top of the stump and stepped well back from the target, looked to Felix and nodded. Felix dropped to one knee, lifted the Sharps to his shoulder, took aim at the target that was well over two hundred yards distant, took a deep breath, let some out and slowly squeezed the trigger. The big rifle boomed, bucked, belched smoke and lead and the .52 caliber slug twisted through the air and smashed into the fist-sized rock, exploding it into a small cloud of white dust.

Felix stood, turned to face the group, "Now, that rock was a mite bigger'n a Injun, but when that Injun is charging you, swinging a tomahawk, and screaming at'chu, you wanna get him stopped and right quick. So, here's what we're gonna do." He motioned to Eustice and Noah, and began instructing the group in the basics of handling, loading and sighting the rifles and pistols, and once satisfied that each one was a little more confident, they began their shooting, each one waiting until one of the instructors was beside them before taking aim and triggering off a round. Most were eager, many were capable, a few were dangerous, and a rare one was exceptional. That rare one was a young lady that was just a whisper above four foot tall and did not appear to weigh much more than the rifle she held, but every time she lifted the weapon, it appeared to be an extension of herself and when she sighted down the barrel and squeezed off a round, she not only hit the target, she hit it dead center every time.

Felix caught Eli's eye and motioned him over. "I want you to watch that redhead girl over there, the little'un. She's some kind o' sharpshooter!" He chuckled.

Eli walked close to the girl, watched as she lifted her Henry .44 rifle and took aim at a branch on a bigger stump, squeezed off her shot and cut the branch off clean. He stepped closer. "That's pretty good shooting. You done any before?"

The girl turned around quickly, surprised at her observer, and answered, "No, sir. Pa never let us girls do any shootin' before."

"Girls?"

"Yessir, I have a little sister, but she's too little to lift a rifle yet."

"I see you have a pistol there. Have you shot it yet?"

"No sir," she answered. "But I'd like to."

"Have at it, but we'll need to move a little closer— over to the right a little, out of the way of the others." He followed her as he motioned for her to lead the way. Once in place, he found a chunk of wood, set it up on a stump, and moved back beside her. Without any instruction, he watched as she loaded the pistol, lifted it and snapped off a quick shot that shattered the chunk of wood. Eli stared at the pieces, looked back at the girl and down at the Remington Army that was just like his, and up at the girl, "You are an exceptional shot, you have that natural ability that few people have."

He sighed heavily, looked at the remains of the chunk of wood that had sat on the stump about fifty yards distant, back to the girl and shaking his head, walked away. He motioned to Felix to wrap up the practice, and the people returned to their wagons to make ready for their nooning.

Eli went to the wagon of Nolan and Ella Thorne, and was invited to share their meal with them, which he gladly accepted. As they sat around the cookfire Eli looked at Nolan and asked, "Have you done any work with your daughter, Clara, as far as using a rifle or pistol?"

The man frowned, glanced to his wife and back to Eli. "No, they've never touched a weapon until now and that's only because you insisted."

Eli grinned, shaking his head and glanced to Clara. "That girl has an unusual ability that I've seldom seen in mature men. She is a natural sharpshooter and could probably outshoot just about anybody on this entire wagon train."

Nolan leaned back, surprised by Eli's revelation, glanced to his daughter and wife, and back to Eli, "Clara?" he asked, quite skeptical. "But, she's never..."

Eli grinned, "It's just an unusual talent or skill and she certainly has it. If we get in a fight, she's the one to have at your side. I doubt if she'd ever miss." He paused, looked at Clara who sat staring. "But there's a bit of difference between shooting stumps and shooting some screaming, attacking, warrior. But what you must always remember, and hopefully you'll never need to do it, but remember, you're not trying to hurt or even kill some-one, you'll only be doing it to protect your family."

She nodded, dropped her eyes to her plate, but Eli continued, "'Course, if you all get hungry and need some fresh meat, she could sure get it for you."

Nolan and his wife, Ella, smiled, looked at their daughter with a newfound pride, and thanked Eli for sharing with them.

———

THEY TOOK to the trail when the sun was high overhead, but black-bottomed clouds were gathering in the north, directly in line with the trail. Although they left the side of the North Platte, the trail took a cut through the hills and soon dropped into a wide basin that sided the river and they made camp at the tree line for some protection from the rising winds. It was with a touch of trepidation that Eli lifted his eyes to the clouds, felt the cool wind on his face, and had the wagons circle up, but pull closer to one another than usual, making a tighter corral for the stock in the middle of the circle. He had experienced storms before and knew how easily the stock could be spooked and scattered and he wanted to be certain that would not happen.

CHAPTER 4

BLIZZARD

The snow came quietly in the night. The wet, heavy snow stealthily blanketed the wide valley that lay between the river and the rising hills that marched into the west, but the hills had disappeared in the downy white of the late spring snow. Eli and Charlie had erected a lean-to of pine boughs, but their fire ring lay hidden beneath the deep snow that showed itself to be well over a foot deep. The animals stood hip shot within the circle of wagons, their heavy winter coats insulating them from the spring surprise. It was the weight of the snow on their blankets that brought both men awake to utter exclamations of surprise and alarm. But the land lay quiet and still, most creatures snuggling under their covers or in their dens and burrows. Nothing moved, even the sky was void of birds as the big snowflakes flittered down, dancing on the still spring air.

But when nature called, the men had to roll from their blankets and pull on their cold footwear, stomp their feet into the boots, and wade deeper into the trees, pushing snow up to their knees. They had tethered their horses beside their lean-to, allowing them shelter under a pair of towering ponderosa that now showed low hanging branches, weighted down with the wet snow. The three horses stood hipshot, nose to tail, and close together, sharing their warmth, yet they paid little attention to the two men wading through the deep snow.

Charlie was first to return to the camp and busied himself with making a cookfire, a little larger than usual, so prompted by the cold that searched through his clothes with icy fingers, probing for a warm spot to coat with icy crystals, but he refused to yield and soon had a blazing fire licking toward the snow clouds and eagerly swallowing the slow drifting flakes that filtered their way downward. Eli grabbed the coffeepot, tried to pour out the dregs and leftover coffee, but the chunk of dark ice refused to move so he placed the pot on the flat rock beside the flames. He shook his head as he stood, hands outstretched to the warmth and glanced toward the wagons to see little movement, but there were a couple cookfires coming to life.

Their breath showing with every move, conversation was kept to a minimum, the men had spent many a camp together and easily shared duties. Eli went to the panniers and brought out the last of a backstrap from a deer taken by Charlie the day before, laid it on a rock near the fire to thaw out enough to slice into broiling thickness for breakfast steaks to go with the cornbread biscuits he was readying for the dutch oven, and the cattail shoots they would be frying. The wagon train would not be moving very early today, if at all, depending on the storm, so it was always best to have a good meal whenever the opportunity presented itself.

The sun had risen high in the morning sky and the storm had let up to show patches of blue sky when Clara

Thorne, the sharpshooter girl, walked into the camp of the two men, cradling her Henry .44 in the crook of her arm and showing a somber expression as she greeted the men. "Morning gentlemen. "

"Well, good morning to you too, Miss Clara," responded Eli. "What brings you away from the wagons on this snowy morning?"

"Didn't know if you noticed we've got comp'ny comin'," she replied with a nod to the south end of the big valley.

Eli frowned, glanced to Charlie, and both men stood from their warm seats on the two logs before the fire and walked away from the camp for a look-see to the south end of the valley. In the distance, about two miles south, several figures showed, moving in a line with horses dragging travois and many riders as well as others walking. It was obviously a village of natives on the move and with families along, it was not a war party or hunting party. Eli looked at Charlie. "What'chu think?"

"Could be Arapaho, Shoshone..." and shrugged. "Think we oughta greet 'em?"

"Prob'ly better, 'fore some o' these pilgrims start takin' pot shots at 'em and raisin' a ruckus. It's too cold to start a fight," suggested Eli, turning back to the horses to saddle up his claybank, Rusty. Charlie told Clara to go back to the wagons, try to keep the people contained and calm and they would go see the natives. The men mounted up, felt their horses hump up a little to show their displeasure at having to leave the warm camp with the thick and warm carpet of pine needles beneath the branches of the ponderosa, but gave in to the men's control and started across the unmarred snowfield, Rusty in the lead and breaking trail.

They were readily spotted, and Eli turned in his

saddle to look back at the wagons and was surprised to see they were difficult to see with the snow-covered bonnets on the wagons and the nearby trees heavily laden with the spring snow. He turned back to look at the approaching villagers and saw it was a sizable village. He guessed about fifty lodges, which would mean about a hundred fifty warriors, maybe two hundred fifty people. As they drew near, the men reined up, held up their right hands, palms forward, and waited for the leaders of the village to approach. Five warriors came close, all bundled in heavy buffalo robes, two of the men, obviously leaders or chiefs, in the lead and both showing a touch of grey in their thick black hair.

They also lifted hands, palms forward, and greeted the two visitors, "Yah-ta-hey!"

Eli and Charlie responded with the same greeting and Eli began, using sign language as he spoke, to explain about the wagon train. "I am called Eli, this is Charlie Two Toes. We are traveling north with the wagon train, going to the land of Three Forks far to the north. These are settlers that want to make their home there, raise their families in peace."

The older of the two leaders nodded, began to respond with a gravelly voice, and in stilted English, which surprised Eli. "I am Oh-has-tee, Hosa, Little Raven, this is Seven Bulls, we are Southern Arapaho. We go north to the Wind River. We go on our first hunt for buffalo. We are at peace with White men. I have been to the land of your great chiefs, and met your chief, Lincoln."

"We thought you were at the Washita with Black Kettle and would go to the Indian territory, Fort Sill."

"We were there, but my people are hungry, and we

came for the buffalo. Then we will go to the land of the people by Fort Sill."

Eli nodded, glanced to Charlie, looked to the chiefs, "Go in peace. May you have a good hunt and take many buffalo for your people."

The chiefs nodded, reined their mounts aside and returned to the head of the long line of villagers bound for the north country. Eli and Charlie watched for a short while, then turned away to return to their camp and report to the people of the wagon train. When they neared the wagons, several of the men were standing between the wagons, rifles in hand, ready for anything but were relieved to see Eli and Charlie ride up with broad grins. Eli looked at Nolan Thorne, Clara standing beside him.

"Looks like we're not gonna have a fight today!" he chuckled, until Clara nodded across the river, "What about them?"

Eli and Charlie turned to look to the low hills beyond the river where a bald saddle showed several horsemen, natives, watching the movement of the village and had probably spotted the wagon train as well. Eli twisted around to retrieve his binoculars from his saddlebags, lifted them for a long look, sighed heavily and handed the field glasses to Charlie. "Looks to be Sioux, mostly young bucks, which means trouble."

Charlie looked, carefully scanning the band, looking for anything that would distinguish the tribe. As he held the glasses to continue to look he said, "Looks to be Oglala, maybe some *Húŋkpapȟa*, hard to tell from here. But you're right, looks to be mostly young bucks, probably lookin' for trouble."

Eli turned to the men, "Then let's get to movin'. The ground's still hard enough we can make it without boggin' down, the snow'll be gone 'fore too long and we can make some time. If those are Sioux, which we're pretty sure they are, then they're allies with the Arapaho, that bunch of villagers. So if they're after a fight or whatever, it'll be us they come after. So, keep your weapons handy, but keep movin'. Charlie'll be out front, but he could use some help..." Eli looked around, "How 'bout you?" He nodded to a young man who appeared to be about sixteen or a little more, "You're Ted Proctor, aren't you?"

"Yessir, I'll go," he volunteered, then looked to his father, Jerry Proctor, a big barrel chested man with thick whiskers who stood next to a little woman that leaned close against him and looked up, fearful for her son, but willing to yield to her man. Jerry glanced to his woman, then to his son, nodded. "Take the grey and the Henry, do what'chur told."

"Yes, Pa," answered an enthusiastic young man turning to fetch his horse.

Eli looked to Nolan Thorne, "How 'bout'chur Clara?"

"She's a girl!" declared a surprised Thorne, looking wide-eyed at Eli.

"She's the best shot in this camp." Eli looked at a grinning Clara who was nodding excitedly.

Thorne looked at Charlie, "Anything happens to her, I'll take it outta yore hide!"

Charlie grinned, "What'chu mean? She's comin' to protect me!" he declared, watching as the girl trotted off to fetch her blood sorrel mare.

Chapter 5

Shadowed

The flats stretched out between the rolling hills and distant flat-top mesas, showing a hint of green that heralded the coming of spring as the grasses, sage, greasewood, and more began to strut their early colors of warm weather. Patches of white marked the lows of the flats that captured the snow and held it for the coming desert blossoms of coneflowers, paintbrush, harebells and blue flax. Eli spotted a patch of locoweed and pointed it out to the lead wagon driven by Thorne, "Keep your animals away from that—it's called locoweed, and it will do just that to your animals."

Thorne nodded, slapped the reins to his mules and kept the wagon moving. The sun was quickly melting the remaining snow and warmed the backs of the animals and riding men. The sky showed blue and promised a warm afternoon as the wagon train began to distance itself from the caravan of natives dragging their travois.

Charlie and his two charges, Clara Thorne and Ted Proctor had taken the lead early and were out of sight of the wagons, having kept to the trail that rode the rolling hills and meandered through the few buttes and hills of the wild country that was dotted with sage, grease wood and scattered juniper and piñon. The naked cottonwoods and aspen, and a few ponderosa lined the banks of the North Platte River, fresh buds doing their best to push through the waxy covering to show their eager green leaves. Charlie spotted a couple mule deer taking a drink in the shallow waters of the dog-leg bend of the river, nodded toward them and spoke to the two young people. "There's a couple deer yonder, but they're pretty common. If we're gonna get a little meat for your folks, let's go a bit further, we might see some desert bighorns that'll offer a change."

"Bighorns?" asked Ted, frowning and glancing at Clara.

"Ummhmm," answered Charlie. "The meat's a little different, good change from the usual, but they're not easy to take. When we see some, you'll need to do just as I say, an' you might learn somethin'."

Clara pushed her mount a little closer to Charlie and asked, "You see those two riders followin' us?" nodding over her right shoulder.

"Yup. They been shadowin' us right along. I reckon they're with that bunch we saw across the river earlier."

"But there's only two of 'em," offered Clara, frowning.

"It's common for any raiding party to have scouts out ahead, sometimes to keep track of their target, some-times to make sure we don't turn and attack them."

"Since there's just the three of us, you think they'll come after us?" asked Clara, concern showing in her eyes and her voice.

"No, prob'ly not. That's why Eli wanted there to be the three of us, just in case. But I think they're just keeping track of us for some reason. I think if they were wanting to hit the wagons, they'd have done it already, 'fore we got to movin'." He nodded to their left, "Let's go up on that butte yonder, have a look around." He reined his buckskin to the left and started toward the saddle between two round-top buttes that stood above the low valley of the North Platte. The butte stood about three hundred feet above the valley floor and overlooked a stretch of flats that showed rust colored with iron ore mixed with the adobe soil giving the appearance of a rumpled orange blanket spread across the grassy flats that held a vast prairie dog village with whistle pigs standing tall and grooming themselves atop the mounds.

Charlie ground tied his buckskin, slipped the binoculars from the saddlebags and looked at the two young people. "Ted, you stay with the horses this time, I'll take Clara. Next time, we'll swap off."

Ted nodded, slipped to the ground and accepted the reins of Charlie's buckskin and Clara's blood sorrel, found a rock to sit on and plopped down to watch the two move in a crouch to the crest of the butte. Once atop, Charlie motioned Clara to get down and follow his example, and proceeded to crawl the rest of the way to the crest of the knob. He bellied down and lifted the binoculars and began a thorough scan of the flats before them.

Slowly moving the glasses from the west to the east, he stopped, watched for a moment, "There's some bighorns. Looks to be a couple good rams, a couple ewes and one lamb." He handed the binoculars to Clara, nodded in the direction of the bighorns, and watched as she had her look. Charlie had exceptional eyesight and searched their backtrail for the two scouts, spotted them as they rode slowly on a parallel trail to the roadway of the Bridger Trail. They had crossed the river and were now on the west bank between the river and the trail where the wagons would pass. But Charlie was certain that the native scouts were more interested in him and the two young people, who were scouting for the wagons, than they were in the wagons, knowing the scouts would be hunting, and taking the same trail of the wagons.

"So the big curl horns are the rams?" asked Clara.

"Yup, but they're tougher than the ewes, but we won't take a ewe with a lamb at her side. We'll ride over to that cluster of rocks on the far side of the trail and far enough away from the sheep so as not to spook 'em. Then we'll see if we can trick 'em to come closer to give you a shot at one of 'em."

Clara frowned, lowered the glasses and looked at Charlie. "Me?"

"Yup, you're a good shot and that might be a little tricky. They can see a whole lot better'n us and they won't get too close, so you'll have to take a long shot."

Clara sighed heavily. "I've never shot anything before," she mumbled, not sure she was willing to kill an animal like that.

———

ELI HAD REINED up to the side of the wagons to watch each one pass and check on the movement of the animals and the wagons. He still had that chill up his spine about the trader's wagons and was uncertain about what was causing his concern, and he was determined to find out the cause or clear his mind of any problem. He watched the wagons pass, noted the condition of all the animals seemed to be good, after all, this was just the second day of their journey and the animals had done little work so far, but it was always good to keep an eye out for any sore feet, open sores from harness, anything that could be easily resolved if caught before it developed into a problem. But it would not be so easy concerning the men and cargo of the trader's wagons, and he leaned on the pommel of his saddle as they neared.

The first two wagons were of the typical prairie schooner style, high sideboards, sloped tailgate, strong wheels, well built out of hardwoods. The canvas bonnets were tied tight, front and back, and the driver and helper sat on the seat, feet on the footboards and nodded and waved as they passed Eli. The third wagon was more of the build of a light-weight freighter, bigger wheels, both in diameter and width, designed to carry heavier loads, similar high sideboards and tailgate, but there was something that bothered Eli and he nudged his horse closer, started to cross the road behind the big wagon and before the next wagon of the trader, but the driver of the next wagon crowded closer and prevented Eli from crossing. Eli pulled back, scowling at the driver who shrugged as if he couldn't help what happened, but Eli looked down at the tracks of the bigger wagon and noticed they were not only wider, but deeper, which told of a heavier than usual load.

Eli waited until the other wagons passed, saw no difference with either of them, and moved across the road to make his way alongside the wagons and back to the front of the line. He ignored the drivers of the freighters as he passed, making a pretense of looking to the hills as if watching for trouble, and went to the head of the line to ride alongside the Thorne wagon. He looked to Thorne, "Seen anything of our scouts?"

"Nothin'. Been wonderin' 'bout 'em though!"

"I'm sure they're fine. Charlie's a good man, he'll make sure they'll be alright. Probably teachin' 'em a little 'bout huntin', maybe gettin' some fresh meat."

"Did you see those Injuns back yonder, two of 'em come across the river an' were ridin' near the trees, looked like they was watchin' us."

"I saw 'em. They're prob'ly scouts for the bigger bunch, tryin' to get a better idea how many fighters we might have 'fore they try anything. But from the number of their bunch, I don't think they'll try to jump a train the size of ours. Just countin' wagon drivers, we got 'em outnumbered two to one, and most natives don't like those kinds of odds."

"I hope you're right," responded Thorne, slapping the reins to his mules to make the grade of a slight rise in the road.

CHAPTER 6

MEAT

The North Platte River tucked itself away into the red rock canyon while the juniper, piñon and scattered scrub cottonwood stood atop the steep walls of the canyon, tempting the lower realms with fleeting shade. The band of bighorns joined another, making the herd number near twenty, mostly ewes and many with lambs at their side. The occasional skeleton of long dead juniper stood with outstretched grey limbs as if warning visitors of the hazards of the steep-walled canyon below, while saddles of grassy flats beckoned wildlife to partake of the spring greens that contrasted with the buffs and browns of last summer's bunch grass. One juniper clung tenaciously to the ledge of the rocks, its roots reaching into nothingness in a desperate attempt at footing or water, disappointed on both counts, but it told of the often despairing efforts for any living thing to hold on to the rarity of life.

Charlie led the two prodigies into the dry wash that lay behind the cluster of rocks set apart from the canyon, but within sight of the grazing herd of bighorns. But movement below the bighorns showed a good bunch of antelope and as he moved slightly, the bighorns scampered higher into the rocks and over the top. He knew they were gone and their best bet for meat was to try for the antelope.

He slipped to the ground, motioned for the two youngsters to do the same, and once below the rocks, he explained the strategy of the hunt. "These antelope have better eyesight and are a little more curious than the Bighorns, so we'll try somethin' different with them. Ted, we'll put this strip of cloth atop your hat, let it blow in the breeze. You'll sit atop the flat rock over the crest, within sight of the herd. You'll need to slowly sneak up to your spot, don't wanna alarm 'em, and slowly lift that cloth to your shoulder, let the breeze catch it and blow as it will, but you need to sit still, don't scratch an itch, don't move your head, nothin'. Got it?"

"Uh, yeah, but what about muh rifle? Won't I need it?"

"Nope," chuckled. "But take it with you, just don't move it." Then turning to look at Clara. "That's where you do your job, Clara. I want you on your belly beside Ted's feet, rifle outstretched before you, but layin' mighty still. Just watch the pronghorns. Purty soon, one or two of 'em will kinda start wanderin' closer, curious like, wantin' to see what that strip of cloth is all about. Now, when one o' them doe without a litt'ln or big belly gets close, or one o' the bucks, young un' preferably with smaller horns, and they get close enough to take a shot, then pull the trigger. But no movin' until then, understand?" he questioned, looking from one to the other.

Both nodded and he motioned for them to take their place, but Ted asked, "What're you gonna do?"

"I'll be keepin' an eye out for those two Sioux warriors, don't want them to mess up our huntin'."

Ted nodded, glanced to Clara and the two started their stealthy climb over the rocks to find their promontory with the flat rock and firing position. Charlie watched them move, pleased with their attempts at stealth, and waited until they were out of sight before turning to the horses and putting out pickets for the three animals. He found a bit of shade under a scrub piñon, stretched out and covered his eyes with his hat and crossed his arms, making ready for a snooze.

Eli rode beside the Thorne wagon and both men kept watching the two Sioux scouts that were riding near the tree line, but also watching the wagons. The big cottonwoods were showing their skeletal branches that would soon burst out in pale-green leaves, but for now held an abundance of buds, that from a distance showed nothing but bare limbs. Scattered aspen stood among the cottonwoods, budding out, but also naked with white bark showing scars of rough winters and trunks scarred by beaver and porcupine.

The sudden report of a rifle shot turned Eli's attention to the two native scouts and saw one held a smoking rifle at his shoulder, the other lifting his, while two young mule deer bucks, one stumbling, the other bouncing away, were trying to flee the attack, but the one fell, and both warriors went to the downed animal.

Eli turned to Thorne, "Looks like they're gettin' meat for the others, or they're tryin' to make it look like that."

He reached back to grab his binoculars to search the terrain along the riverbank for any sign of the rest of the band of native warriors. He knew there would be no dust for a giveaway, what with the earlier snowfall, but he watched for any movement and soon spotted figures riding through the thinner aspen growing on the far side of the river. The timber was too thick to give a good look, but the movement told of a good-sized war party, he guessed at least twenty, probably twice that many, and they were paralleling the wagon train, continuing to move north along the river. Eli lowered the field glasses, shook his head and breathed heavily, glanced to Thorne, "I'm gonna pass the word back along the other wagons for everyone to keep their weapons handy. I don't think they're gonna attack anytime soon, but they're waiting for something, maybe another band to join them and improve their numbers, but we still need to be ready. If you get the word, don't hesitate to circle up the wagons, and pull 'em close. Keep the animals inside and stack anything you can between the wagons for cover."

"Will do," responded a somber Nolan Thorne, glancing to his wife Ella.

She looked to Eli, "What about Clara?"

Eli grinned, "She's prob'ly safer'n the rest of us. Charlie'll see to that!" he declared as he reined the big claybank around to start down the line of wagons and pass the word. As he passed each wagon, he directed the drivers to keep their weapons handy and for any others of their wagon to do the same. "We don't know if they plan on doing anything, but it's best to be ready. If you get the order, circle up and do it quick, keep 'em close and the animals inside."

Each driver acknowledged the orders with a nod and a glance to their womenfolk, a look to their nearby weapons for reassurance, and a slap on the rumps of their animals to keep up the pace. When he neared the freighters, each man nodded, some lifted their weapons to show their readiness, and they kept the wagons moving. When he reached the last wagon, Eli reined around and started toward the front of the line, keeping between the wagons and the river, always watching the movement of the two scouts and for any movement on the far bank. When he spotted the band of warriors start across the river, Eli kicked the claybank into a gallop and motioned to the wagons as he passed to pick up the pace.

When he came alongside the Thorne wagon, "Get 'em movin'! The war party's crossin' the river—we need to get to the hills for better cover 'fore we circle up!"

He dug heels to the claybank and stretched out ahead of the wagons. The terrain before them showed rolling hills but he wanted more cover, maybe a tall butte or thicker timber.

———

THE CRACK of the rifle shot brought Charlie instantly awake and on his feet, rifle in hand. A quick scan showed nothing near, but the second rifle shot came from over the crest of the rocky upthrust. He took the mound in three long bounds, saw both Ted and Clara standing, rifles in hand and looking beyond them where two downed antelope lay, the rest of the herd bounding away in long strides without a look behind.

Charlie chuckled, walked up behind the pair of first-time hunters and said, "Good shootin', one each?"

Both young people nodded and Ted said, "She got the first one, just like you said, and I got the second one. My trigger finger was itchin' and I thought she'd never shoot, but soon's she did, I brought mine up and got the second one just as he turned away. Lucky shot, I reckon, he was about to hightail it outta here!"

Charlie chuckled, lowered his rifle, "Now the work

begins," and started to the downed animals. He stood over the first one and was surprised to hear a gunshot from back along the river, but it was a single shot and a good distance away. He waited for any additional shooting, but none came, and he guessed it was another hunter probably taking one of the two mule deer they saw earlier. He dropped to one knee, motioned the two young people to do the same, and as he withdrew his Green River knife, he began explaining the process of field dressing the animals. When the two hunters took over, Charlie went to retrieve the horses and as he crested the rocky mound, he heard the distant sounds of wagons, but they were moving fast and that was unusual.

CHAPTER 7

SURVEILLANCE

The Sioux war party kicked up their horses to keep pace with the wagons, but not to overtake them. Eli had spotted a suitable place for defense, dropped back and told Thorne where to go and to circle the wagons, then pulled back and told every ten wagons to pick up the pace and move alongside the others, making three parallel lines for defense while on the move. As the wagons passed, he looked back toward the tail end of the line and saw the five freighters pulling off to the side. He frowned, reined the claybank around and went back to the wagons, saw Felix Carpenter, the sergeant from the 10th, pulling up on his team and Eli moved alongside. "What's the matter? Why you stoppin'?"

Felix leaned out to look at his left front wheel. "Hear that? 'Bout to lose that wheel. If we don't stop and fix it, we'll lose the whole wagon!" he declared as he leaned back on the lines. The other freighters were pulling up close and Catlin called out to Felix, "What's happenin'?"

"The wheel!" hollered Felix, wrapping the lines

around the brake handle and beginning to step down. He looked at the wheel, saw the hub smoking and turned to Catlin. "I'll need some help! We'll hafta pull the wheel, grease the axle and hub!"

Catlin stood, leaned around and hollered to the others, "You men give him a hand! We gotta get that fixed 'fore them Injuns attack!" motioning to the war party that was still near the trees but keeping pace with the wagons.

Catlin looked at Eli, "What do you want us to do? We can't leave the wagon, they'll strip it!"

"Have half your men stand around the wagon with rifles in hand, let the others fix the wheel, and come along when you can. I'll try to get some others to come back and help!"

Catlin nodded and Eli reined Rusty around and took off at a gallop to catch up with the rest of the wagons. When he came alongside Thorne's wagon that was still in the lead, he hollered and pointed. "Pull to that draw 'tween those buttes. Instead of circling, we'll make a square and space out the center for the teams. When we get stopped, if they haven't hit us yet, we'll put some of the better shooters on the crests of the buttes behind the wagons!"

———

CHARLIE, leading the horses behind him, returned to the two shooters, "We'll cut 'em down, cut the legs and heads off, put 'em on behind your saddles, and get back to the wagons. Somethin's happenin' and we need to get back." They wasted little time gutting and cutting the carcasses of the antelope, tying a carcass on behind Ted's saddle and the second behind Clara's saddle. They mounted up and with Charlie leading, started back to the wagons at a lope. Within moments, Charlie saw the wagons coming toward them, but turn off the road to make for the line of buttes to the west of the trail. He spotted Eli riding alongside the lead wagon, shouting and motioning to the drivers. A quick glance told Charlie what Eli had in mind and he motioned to the two young riders to stay close, and he pointed his buckskin to the long slope of the buttes, making for the crest that would overlook the long draw that appeared to be the target for the wagons.

The three riders kept to their saddles and coaxed the horses up the climb of the buttes and within moments, they made the crest of the first butte that held a scattering of juniper. Charlie motioned them down and all three hit the ground, loosely holding the reins and Charlie pointed out the wagons and the Sioux war party beyond. "They're taking cover from the Sioux! I want you two to find cover there"—pointing to a rocky abutment just below the crest of the butte— "and there"— motioning to a cluster of piñon and rocks a little closer to the cut between the buttes that held the long draw where the wagons were forming up. "Ted, you take the rocks, and Clara, you take the trees, but keep your head down behind those rocks. Don't do any shooting unless the war party hits the wagons and then pick your shots carefully. I'm gonna be just across that cut in those rocks yonder," motioning to a cluster of boulders that shouldered the near butte about a hundred yards from their current location. "If you get into any trouble, fire a shot my direction, just don't hit me, and wave me over. I'll hot-foot it back right away." He looked around, looked at the two. "Tether your horses behind the trees here, keep an eye out just in case any of 'em try to come around behind us, and if nothing happens about dusk, I'll come back after you and we'll join the wagons."

Both the young people looked at one another, then to Charlie and nodded as they started to tether their mounts when Charlie mounted his buckskin and started for his chosen promontory that would overlook the wagons. He hoped their positions would give the added advantage for the defense of the wagons. He did not like leaving the young people, but he had confidence in them and knew many their age were already on their own and they had already proven themselves with the taking of the antelope.

———

THE WAGONS of the freighters had drawn close to one another, offering cover and some protection if they were attacked and Felix and his two fellow soldiers set to work quickly and efficiently, using a spare tongue as a lever to lift the weight off the problem wheel and remove the lynch pin to remove the wheel. While Eustice crawled under the front end to grease the bolsters and Felix and Noah with Skunk Hoxie removed the wheel as Felix began greasing the metal thimble and the inside of the hub. Dre Jackson, Bucky Fields, Elias Hamilton, and Chuck Kappler stood around the wagons, rifles in hand, watching the distant band of natives as Catlin mounted his horse and started to a low knoll that stood lonely just west of the trail. Felix caught a glimpse of the trader as he rode away and watched him for a moment, frowning and wondering, but quickly returned his attention to the necessary repairs.

The experienced freighters finished their repairs, lowered the wagon to the ground and within moments, all were aboard and the five freighters whipped their teams to a trot and followed the rest of the wagons where they left the trail and soon joined the square formation, filling in the spaces on the close corner with their five wagons, unhitching the teams and turning them into the center of the wagons while the men helped arrange gear and boxes for cover between the wagons, several keeping watch for any coming attack.

Eli was making the rounds, encouraging everyone, offering suggestions for firing positions, and for some of the women that were not too sure about using a weapon, to ready themselves and the ammunition for reloading. Once he made the rounds, Eli swung back aboard Rusty and headed for the crest of the tallest butte behind the wagons, having seen Charlie take up his position, but he wanted high ground to watch the natives and to be ready for any coming attack.

The line of buttes formed a horseshoe basin that held the wagons, but there was ample space between the wagons and the buttes for firing at any attackers that might try to get close. There was little ground cover, a few scattered sage, greasewood, some yucca, but nothing in abundance that offered cover for any attackers, and Eli, once atop the butte that rose high above the basin, was afforded a view of the trail, and open space between the line of hills and the distant river and the thickets of trees that sided the water. He was confident they had a good position, but the natives had not commenced any attack, yet still shadowed the wagons and now were gathered in a slight swale near the trail, a low spot that afforded them cover in the distance, and it appeared they might be making a camp. The two scouts had returned to the band with their fresh kill, and they were making a cook fire.

Eli watched the band with his binoculars, although the butte he was on where he sat in the shadow of a lone juniper, was no more than a hundred feet higher than the camp of the wagons below, he did have a good line of sight to the warriors. As he watched, he saw two lone warriors come from further back down the trail and join the others, but these were not the scouts they had spotted previously. Eli frowned, trying to guess just what they were planning, *I wonder if they had circled around behind these buttes, looking for a way to attack from behind us.* Then he saw a lone rider, not a native come from a low dry ravine and join the wagons. He wasn't certain, but he thought it might be Catlin. *Now, what's he up to?*

Eli lowered the binoculars, looked at the lowering sun, and stood, caught Charlie's attention, and motioned for them to return to the wagons. He mounted up and started back to the formation below, met Charlie as he and the two hunters were showing off their fresh meat and sharing it with others, and drew Charlie to the side. "Let's you and me make camp up top those buttes. I was gonna have several of the men take turns standing watch up there, but if you and I stay up there, we can do it better. There's something going on that I'd like to do a little checkin' on."

Chapter 8

Suspicion

Dusk dropped its curtain without any activity from the Sioux. From the promontory on the buttes, Eli and Charlie could see the warriors making camp, with no movement that would show an anticipated attack. The horses were picketed below the camp in the lower end of the dry ravine, watched over by two of the younger wannabe warriors. It promised to be a cloudless night, the coolness of the early spring weather driving most deep into their blankets, and the moon waxing to half offered ample light for Charlie and Eli, both of whom had protected their night vision with no campfire. As the night lights lit their lanterns and the moon rose a little higher, Eli watched the valley below. Campfires winked into the night among the wagons, shadows moved near the bonneted wagons, but there was no gaiety, music, or loud conversations. Darker shadows showed between the wagons as armed men were posted to watch into the night.

Charlie came near Eli, spoke softly, "Anything happenin'?"

"Nothin' unusual, folks finishin' their supper an' such," answered Eli.

A rattle of rocks brought their attention to the lower flank of the butte until a low voice came. "Comin' up to ya, Colonel." It was the voice of Felix Carpenter, the sergeant from the 10th Cavalry. "Don't shoot me, got sumpin' to tell ya."

And in the same tones, Eli answered, "I hear ya, c'mon up."

The branches of the juniper pushed aside and the big man with a wide grin came through. "Evenin', Colonel," chuckled Felix, moving closer and sitting on the edge of a big boulder.

"So, what brings you up here, Felix?"

"Sumpin' I think you should know about." He took a deep breath, looked below to the wagons. "Catlin don' know I'm up here an' I'd be in some kinda trouble if'n he was to know, but earlier when muh wagon had some trouble, you know, you saw it, well, after you left, Catlin took off on horseback by his ownself, back down the trail an' over the little hill what put him outta sight. He was gone a good while—we fixed the wagon and such, got back on the trail after the rest of 'em, an' it was a while later when he come back to join us. Never said nuthin'. Then when we was parkin' the wagons, I was up on the driver's seat, lookin' back, and way back yonder the natives was gatherin' up in the draw and two lone riders came from the same direction as Catlin an' joined up with the rest o' them natives."

"So, you think Catlin had a meetup with the natives?"

"Ummhmm, an' I dunno if'n you noticed, but that one bigger wagon's a mite heavier than the rest, an' he don' let nobody get anywhere near it cep'n the driver and roustabout what's allus with it."

"So, you're prob'ly thinkin' the same thing I am, he's tradin' rifles to the Sioux."

Felix grinned, nodding his head. "Dunno what else'd make him so secretive."

"We can't be lettin' that happen. Putting rifles into the hands of a bunch of renegade Sioux, especially young bucks wantin' to earn honors an' such, that would mean the death of a lot of settlers, gold miners, just about anyone other than the Sioux."

"Ummhmm. And we din't spend them years in uniform fightin' them savages an' losin' friends to be lettin' that happen. Just can't do it," responded Felix, shaking his head and looking below to the gathered wagons where campfires were dimming and movement settling down as the families and others made ready for bed.

Felix looked up at Eli, "Colonel, Catlin said that wagon had some o' that new explosive called dynamite in it and that's why he was so protective of it, but the wagon I'se drivin' has several boxes what's marked the same. I took a look, an' them sticks is the same as what the army was testin' back to Fort Hays just 'fore we left —it was new then. Catlin says it's sumpin' they be usin' in the minin' of gold an' such. He says it be better'n reg'lar blastin' powder. They puts a little cap, bigger'n the ones used on rifles an' such, into the end of the stick, stuffs a fuse in it, an' lights the fuse then run like the devil's after yo 'cuz when it blows up it do make a mess."

"So, what're you thinkin', Felix?"

"Mebbe we could use some o' whut's in my wagon to blow up th' other wagon."

Eli looked at Felix, glanced to Charlie. "Sounds mighty dangerous to me."

"Ummhmm, but so's the idee o' them guns gittin' in the hands o' them Sioux."

"When you thinkin'?" asked Eli.

"Gotta be soon, them natives'll be gittin' tired o' waitin'. He'll prob'ly make some excuse for that wagon to drop back or sumpin', but if'n I could get a couple sticks under that wagon, a long fuse, then all I'd need to do is light it an' run!"

"But if you were seen, or too many people around…" Eli shrugged, shaking his head.

"Wal, I won' do it if'n you don' want, but if'n you do, I'll sneak down there tonight when nobody's thinkin' 'bout nothin' but gettin' attacked. I'll make up the charge, tie it unner the wagon box, stretch the fuse where I can get to it, and…" He shrugged, grinning.

Eli looked at Charlie. "What do you think?"

"I don' know nuthin' 'bout no dynamite or blastin' powder. If'n it ain't got a trigger, well…" He shrugged, glancing from Eli to Felix and back.

Eli looked to Felix, "You go ahead and try to do what you said, but don't go gettin' yourself in a jam. Charlie and I will see what else we can do to hold up the Sioux, keep 'em off the wagons. I'll be down with the wagons shortly. I wanna let folks know we'll be headin' out at first light an' they might hafta do without breakfast or so, but that might get Catlin to make his move with the natives."

Felix stood, nodded, and started back down the slope to make his way to the wagons. He hoped to get back to his wagon before he was missed so he wouldn't raise any suspicion. As Felix disappeared into the deepening shadows, Eli turned to Charlie. "Think we could get the horses away from the natives?"

Charlie let a slow grin paint his face and shook his

head, "You're just bound and determined to get us into trouble, aren't you?" he chuckled. He looked at Eli, thinking about what he proposed, turned to look in the direction of the wagons and the distant camp of the Sioux. "We might get close by usin' that dry gulch yonder, it'll take a while and we'd hafta do it on foot, but they usually have the younger inexperienced bucks watch the horses and they usually fall asleep long 'bout midnight. That'd be the time we get there, an' if we can do it, mebbe just knock 'em out an' not spook the horses, mebbe..." he shrugged.

"Then let's walk through the wagons like we're checkin' on folks, then slip off into the darkness and head that way. I want the folks to maybe put together some biscuits and such for their breakfast that they can eat on the trail, so we get an early start. That way if we're successful with the horses, we'll put some distance 'tween us an' them, and it'll give Felix time to do his deed, hopefully."

"And if he can't?"

"Then we'll hafta check out the wagons ourselves and do what we think is right."

Charlie chuckled, stood, and gathered up his gear to pack back aboard his horse, they would keep them rigged up and tethered inside the wagons while they made their foray to the camp of the natives. If they had to make a quick getaway, the horses would be ready and all they would need to do is tighten the girths, swing aboard, and hit the trail.

They picked their way through the rocks and brush as they made their way down the slope of the hills to the wagons, entered the formation of the wagons and began making their rounds, Charlie going one way, Eli the other. They soon met at the lower end of the wide draw where the wagons were nestled, and just past the last of the wagons of the trader. With nothing more than a nod, the two men faded into the darkness and started for the moonlit draw that went from the buttes to the river and held the campsite of the natives, situated about a mile and a half from the wagons. Both men wore moccasins, carried only their holstered handguns, and would be dependent on their knives, Eli with his big razor sharp Bowie that lay in the sheath between his shoulder blades, and Charlie with his Green River in the scabbard at his hip. They preferred to take the horses without letting any blood, but the lives of the families with the wagons, and the many settlers that were dependent on the peace treaty between Red Cloud's Oglala and the soldiers of Fort Laramie, would take precedence if necessary. And this was a mission to prevent the arming of young bucks and renegades bent on earning war time honors and gaining coups and scalps, perhaps bounty in the form of stolen horses, and other goods as well as gaining a weapon like the repeating rifles of the soldiers, that would give them status among their people when they strutted with the fresh scalps of white settlers and gold seekers.

CHAPTER 9

CONFLICT

The two moved quietly through the sandy-bottomed gulch, working closer to the encampment of the Sioux, yet all the while, Eli was bothered at the unusual move of the natives to camp so close and within sight of the wagons. It was their normal practice to make an isolated and well-protected encampment, well away from any sight that might become a battleground, yet they were boldly camped near the wagons, as if daring the settlers or threatening the settlers, making them uneasy, on-edge, and nervous.

As they neared the mouth of the draw, the pale moonlight showed their encampment that lay in the slight basin with several piñon and juniper around, with the horse herd further down the wide draw and spread out on the grassy flat. Off to their left, a slight mound lifted from the darkness, showing its bald top to the moonlight and beckoning the predators to make their assault by moving to the back side of the low butte and approaching the herd and the guards from the south with the moon still at their backs. Shadows moved in silhouette near the coals of their cookfire, low grumbles came as the movers spoke quietly among themselves.

Charlie suggested, "I oughta get closer, see what they're plannin'."

"You understand Sioux?"

"Mostly, it ain't that much different from our language an' the Cheyenne."

"I'll wait," answered Eli, glancing to the moon and the few shadowy clouds. "But don't take long. We need to get to the horses 'fore too long."

Charlie grinned and disappeared into the shadows, moving quickly but silently. He kept the bigger junipers between his approach and the sleeping forms, and dropped to all fours as he neared. The few figures that sat near the coals of the cookfire were speaking softly, but the night air carried their conversation, at least enough to be heard and mostly understood by Charlie. Within moments, he heard what he needed and slipped away, returning to the side of Eli.

"What'd you learn?" asked Eli, whispering into the night.

"That they're plannin' on getting a load of rifles from the trader sometime tomorrow. They're already makin' plans for a raid on the gold camp near South Pass, after they take the wagon train. The trader's expectin' to be paid in gold, they'll pay him in blood and take the rest of the wagons also."

A simple nod from Eli told Charlie the new direction of their approach and the two men, still moving in a low and slow crouch, rose from the draw to take to the back side of the low butte. Once out of sight and hearing of the Sioux, Charlie pointed to the shoulder of the butte. "Let's go up there, that'll give us a view of both the camp and the herd, might make it easier."

Eli nodded and followed Charlie as he moved through the low shadows of sage, greasewood, and rabbitbrush to make the crest of the shoulder. As they came to the rise, both men dropped to their bellies and crawled to the crest to begin their survey of the land.

Charlie whispered, "Looks to be more'n we thought. I'd guess a good forty or more."

"Ummhmm, but look yonder at the herd. Looks to be three, maybe four guards and with no big trees, they look to be near sage or brush. I'd say four, one on the far side by the edge of the draw, keepin' 'em from goin' down toward the road, another'n by that cluster of sage, maybe two, one yonder under those rocks, and the fourth closer to us below that lip of the embankment."

Charlie nodded. "I'll take this close'n an' those two by the sage. You take them others, an' I'll give you a little time to get closer to the first one. We'll hafta silence 'em for certain, horses'll spook otherwise."

Charlie watched as Eli slowly worked his way to the bottom of the narrow gulch, rose to the other side, and started toward the first of the guards that sat near the cluster of rocks that offered him a slight promontory of the herd, most standing hipshot, heads hanging. Eli disappeared in the darkness and Charlie started off the shoulder toward the guard that was sitting just under the embankment of the draw, almost directly below him. He moved quietly and intermittently, using even the slightest clump of grass or bit of brush for cover, until he approached the lip of the embankment. He paused, listening and heard the regular breathing of the young man that told of his sleeping, his chin on his chest, as he leaned back against the clay embankment. Charlie moved back, dropped over the edge of the embankment and came at the guard from the shadows. With one stealthy move, he stepped up the clay bank, put his left hand over the mouth of the guard and drew the narrow blade of the knife across his throat. The man tried to kick, but the spurting blood choked him, and he went limp with death. Charlie held his hand on his mouth until certain the man was dead, then pushed his head back against the embankment, folded his arms across his chest, giving the body the appearance of sleep. Charlie wiped the blade and his hands in the loose dirt, and moved away, rising to the crest of the embankment and starting for the cluster of sage where one or two others snoozed.

Eli had little cover, mostly sage and yucca, but he used every clump and cluster as well as shadows from tall grass or rises in the ground, always moving in a low crouch, often on all fours. He neared the cluster of rocks from the far side, on the high ground, and as he drew close, each move slower than before, every footstep carefully placed, the few sounds of the night from nighthawks, cicadas, crickets and coyotes, used to cover his moves. Eli slipped the Bowie from the sheath, held it at his side, and moved to the rocks. He paused, listening, heard nothing but the occasional gasp or snort that told him the man was snoozing if not asleep, and carefully moved to the edge of the rocks for a better look.

The figure of the young man showed to be full-grown, well-muscled, with a roach head piece and a hair pipe bone breastplate, but his arms were crossed over his chest and his chin rested on his chest and he snorted and snored. Eli used the rocks and crawled closer, reached down from above and behind the man, put his left hand over his nose and mouth and slit his throat with the big-bladed Bowie, the knife so sharp and the cut so deep, he almost decapitated the man. The warrior made one kick, tried to grab at the knife, but blood spilled on his hands and over his chest, taking the life of the warrior to pour into the ground. Eli held tight, until no movement nor strength could be felt, and slowly released his hold. The body started to slide to the side, but he dropped from the rocks, sat the body back against the stone and sat in the shadows to clean the blade, when he heard a voice call softly into the darkness, *"Khoka! Khoka!"*

Eli froze in place, slowly melting into the shadow of the rocks, looking to see another warrior coming from nearer the horses and calling out to the dead guard. He called again, *"Khoka!"* and stepped closer, slowly drawing his knife from the sheath at his side and dropping into a crouch. But he had moved only a step closer when the big Bowie whispered through the air from an under-handed throw from Eli and buried itself in the low chest of the warrior, who stopped, dropped his own knife, and fell to his knees as he grabbed at the big knife impaled in his chest. He lifted wide eyes to the shadows and Eli stepped forward, letting the dying man see his slayer. The warrior fell to his face in the dirt, to paint the clay red with his blood and never move again. Eli moved closer, pushed at him with his foot and receiving no response, rolled the man to his back and retrieved his knife, wiping it clean on the buckskin leggings of the dead warrior.

Charlie worked his way to the sage cluster where the other one or two guards were last seen, carefully made his approach in the shadows and lay quiet, listening, knowing if there were two and they were awake, they would talk, but he heard only the restless sounds of a man trying to get comfortable to sleep. As the movement stopped, Charlie, now on his belly, slithered toward the sage and paused, watched the dim moonlit figure and knew he had dozed. Charlie rose, stepped closer and quickly sent the warrior to join his ancestors as quietly as the others.

Eli dropped into his crouch, moved among the sage and yucca toward the lower end of the draw where the guard was last seen, and searched the shadows for any sign of the man. He moved to another sage, dropped to his knees and searched the rolling terrain, brush, and the bottom of the dry gulch, but nothing moved save a few horses that occasionally snorted, lifted their heads, and shifted their weight. Eli came to his feet, moved in his crouch and made a better search, thinking the second guard he killed near the first, was probably the one they had seen at the bottom end of the gulch. After a fruitless search, he moved back among the horses, speaking softly, touching them, and used a rawhide reata taken from the guard to put a half-hitch halter on the head of one dark bay horse that showed little sign of concern. He led the horse to the edge of the herd, gave the cry of a night hawk, *peent, peent,* to signal Charlie and was soon answered.

Eli saw Charlie swing aboard a horse, give a wave and they started the herd moving, slowly at first, but when the animals grew restless, they shouted a war cry and the herd jumped as if joined together and took off at a full gallop down the draw, away from the encampment of the Sioux.

Eli was nearer the front of the herd and as they approached the wagon road, he waved, shouted, and nudged the leaders to turn them south along the roadway. Charlie continued to push the small herd, but kept watch over his shoulder, knowing there were always a few warriors that kept their favorite war pony at their side and would quickly give chase. He had seen at least two animals at the encampment when he crept near, and he knew they would be coming. He lay low on the neck of his mount, keeping a low profile yet waving and shouting to drive the herd. He twisted around to see two warriors giving chase and with a quick glance to the flanks of the hills beside the road, he nudged his mount into the few juniper and reined up, drawing his pistol and watching the warriors come charging on. As they passed, riding in the dust cloud of the fleeing herd, Charlie kicked his mount into the dust and came up behind the two warriors, as he came alongside the first one, he lifted his pistol, but instead of shooting the man, he brought the barrel down on the back of the man's head, knocking him from his mount to crumple in the dust.

Charlie dug heels into the ribs of his mount, coming up behind the second warrior, saw him lift a rifle and take aim toward Eli, and Charlie dropped the hammer on the pistol, sending the lead slug chasing the warrior as the pistol roared, bucked and spat a line of fire in the dust and darkness. The warrior fell to the neck of his horse, slid off the side, and his mount continued the chase after the herd.

CHAPTER 10

BREAKAWAY

Nolan Thorne and Mark Ryan had been voted in as co-captains of the wagon train before they left Fort Laramie and Eli had taken the men into his confidence regarding their suspicions of the trader Catlin and Eli's plan for him and Charlie to try to run off the horse herd. When the men heard the gunshots from the darkness, they quickly rousted the rest of the men, and everyone quickly set about harnessing the horses and mules. When Catlin was told he groused around a bit, but had no choice but to get his men busy with the teams and wagons. Felix watched the trader talking with Dre Jackson, his ramrod, as they walked to the far side of the big wagon. Felix shook his head, watching, and thinking *I sure hope I got that fuse tucked away so they can't see it, hate to get caught now.* But the men were busy with their plans and paid little attention to the wagon, thinking as most outlaws do, believing they know more than anyone else and can out-smart everyone, never thinking that someone might know what they were planning.

It was less than an hour later when Nolan Thorne slapped the reins to the rumps of his team of mules and started the wagons back to the Bridger Trail wagon road that sided the North Platte. The sky in the east silhouetted the rolling hills as it turned the black of night into the blend of blue and grey that banded the eastern sky, presaging the coming of the morning sun. And with the light behind them, the fading moonlight before them, they watched the stars begin to snuff their lanterns as the long shadows of early morning stretched across the road.

The train had lined out on the road when Eli and Charlie came riding up at a gallop aboard the Indian ponies and dropped to the ground beside their horses that were hitched to the back of Thorne's wagon, already saddled and geared up. Both men quickly slipped the lead lines from the tailgate, tightened the girths on the saddles and mounted up, slapped the native mounts on the rump to send them running, and with a nod to Thorne, Charlie took to the lead to scout and Eli pulled off to the side to watch the wagons pass, waiting for Mark Ryan's wagon that was the last of the settlers wagons before the five wagons of the trader.

Eli pulled alongside the Ryan coach, twisted around on his seat to look back at the trader's wagons to see Felix driving the lead wagon, and give Eli a nod and a grin. Eli reined Rusty to the side, well off the trail to climb a slight shoulder that would give him a good view of their back trail that was beginning to show its twisting ribbon of road in the morning sun. As he watched, he noticed the bigger wagon of the trader had dropped back a little and the driver was standing, looking about, feigning some sort of problem. He reined up, called to the wagon ahead and motioned them to keep going, then climbed down from the seat. Eli detected a wisp of smoke at the rear of the wagon that would not be seen by the driver, unless he walked to the back, but the driver moved between the team of mules and the wagon, bending over to do something with the harness or running gear. Eli started to go to see if he could help, but remembering the plan of Felix, hesitated and watched.

The wisp of smoke faded and just as the driver was pulling the team away from the wagon, a massive explosion shook the ground, raised a huge cloud of dust and debris, and wood, canvas, and other debris soared into the sky and began falling to the ground around the massive hole that was all that remained of the wagon. Eli had taken a firm grip on the reins of his stallion, but the big horse spooked, reared up and pawed at the empty sky, almost unseating Eli before dropping down and try to tuck his head between his front feet, but Eli held firm, kept the horse's head up, keeping him from taking off or trying to buck him off, and as soon as he began to settle, Eli bent down and stroked his neck, talking softly to reassure the trembling horse.

The driver, Chuck Kappler, had held fast to the lines of the team and was being dragged by the six-up, yet refusing to let loose the lines. Eli spotted Catlin coming back at a gallop, eyes wide and waving away the dust with his hat, searching the roadway for any remnants of the cargo. Eli watched the man, who had not even noticed Eli, ride past, and chuckled at the success of Felix's plan. Eli nudged Rusty forward, following Catlin, and as he neared, he looked at Catlin, "What happened? What'd you have in that wagon?"

"Dunno what happened. I did have some o' that new explosive dynamite in there, thought the miners in the gold camp would like to have some of it. Maybe it got jostled around too much. It's still pretty new, you know, anything coulda happened." He looked at Eli, back to the crater and the scattered debris, shaking his head.

Eli, looking about, "Looks like there were some rifles in that wagon, there's some stocks and barrels layin' yonder, course they're not any good now, but there's no fixin' them, that's for sure."

"Yeah, I had some rifles in there, you know, the settlers and miners always need rifles for huntin' and such. They were left from the war, got 'em cheap, thought I'd make a few dollars on 'em, but not now."

Eli leaned on the pommel of his saddle, crossing his arms and looked at Catlin, and slowly shook his head. "Look, Catlin, we know you were trying to make a deal with those natives. That's why we ran off their horses, and as far as your rifles and such, if you would have traded them to the Sioux, the soldiers at Fort Fetterman would have put you in irons. So, if you're smart, you won't have anything more to do with them, but they might come looking for you and I'm not going to endanger any of those settlers for your greed, so you best watch your step. Got it?"

"Uh, uh, I wasn't makin' any deal with the natives, really I wasn't!" replied a jittery Catlin, his confidence gone and his fear showing across his florid face.

"We heard the natives talking about the deal they were making with you and that they were expecting to get delivery of the rifles today. Then they planned on killing you and your men and everybody else on the wagon train." Eli shook his head, his disgust showing in his tone and his expression. He spat on the ground, grumbled, "Just remember what I said. You and all your wagons are not worth the life of one of those settlers!" He reined around the big claybank and took off after the wagons, remembering that Catlin hadn't even asked about the driver of the wagon.

Eli caught up with Mark Ryan. "That's the end of his gun running for now, no need to tell the others, just that he had a blowup of some blasting powder he planned on selling to the miners."

Mark nodded, slapped reins to the team and watched as Eli rode ahead, passing the wagons, answering those that asked, but kept from stopping, intent on making it to the lead wagon and report to Nolan Thorne. Once he told Nolan, he added, "I'm goin' on up ahead, catch up to Charlie, see if we can get some fresh meat for the families."

Nolan called out, grinning, "Uh, those two young hunters, as they call themselves, Clara and Ted, already took out after him. They're planning on doing just that!"

Eli chuckled, "Then I'll find a good promontory, have a good look around. Make sure there's no more natives up to mischief!"

Nolan nodded, and Eli started off toward the low-rising buttes just west of the trail where the river began to make a wide bend to the west and the terrain was taking on a look of more hills, thicker sage and more cacti like the prickly pear, hedgehog, yucca and cholla. It was beginning to show itself as the foothills of the mountains and they would soon see the different mountain ranges like the Big Horns in the north, the smaller Owl Creek mountains in the northwest, and the western-most range known as the Wind River mountains that painted the western horizon and cradled the setting sun at the end of the day, but that was a considerable distance and several days travel away.

When the North Platte began to hug the hills on the south, the trail crossed over the river on a gravel bottomed crossing and followed the meandering river on the north bank. It was a long day's travel when they passed Bed Tick Creek and neared Antelope Creek where the road would cross back to the south side of the now northbound river. They made camp in the cottonwoods near the riverbank, and everyone looked forward to a leisurely supper and a good night's sleep, but Eli would not allow them to let their guard down and assigned guard duty to most of the men on two hour shifts. He was not certain the war party of Sioux would give up on their chase, and was determined to have a well-protected train.

CHAPTER 11

WESTWARD

"Greater love hath no man than this, that a man lay down his life for his friends." Began Parson Shadrach Spencer. "That's from the book of John, chapter 15 and verse 13."

The parson had been asked by the people to have a Sunday morning service before the wagon train pulled out to continue their journey, and with a little hesitation and concern regarding the possible retaliation by the natives, Eli agreed with the condition that the parson try his best to make it short. Parson Shadrach nodded and grinned and stepped behind the stack of boxes that had been fashioned into a pulpit and opened his Bible to motion to the people to gather around and make themselves comfortable.

After beginning with the recited verse, he continued. "We've all known of times when someone has given his life for a friend, a family member, a fellow soldier or others. We've also known of times when someone has put his life on the line to protect others, or taken some dangerous risk to keep others safe. We've seen it with men among this crowd this morning, and we will probably see it again. But I would like us to think back a little further, back to the time when one man willingly laid down his life for many. That man was none other than the Son of God, Jesus. He had lived a sinless life, performed many amazing miracles, even raised one man from the dead, then to fulfill the plan of God, he stretched out his arms on the cruel wooden cross, and watched as soldiers drove spikes into his palms and his feet, lifted the cross high and dropped it into the hole in the ground to jar every bone in Jesus's body out of joint, and still he looked around and said, *Father, forgive them, for they know not what they do."* The parson paused, looking at those before him, some seated on blankets, some on boxes, others on the ground.

He stepped back behind the makeshift pulpit and scanned the crowd. "Now, why would He do such a thing? Because the *wages of sin is death!* Romans 6:23. Because we are sinners, the penalty for that sin is death and that penalty must be paid! So Christ, in His love for us, stepped up and offered his life to pay that price and by doing that, He purchased for us the gift of eternal life." He paused again and looked at each one. "So my question for you is, 'Have you accepted that gift of eternal life?' If you have, great, then we can know we'll be in Heaven forever together. But if you haven't, remember He, Jesus, has paid the price for you to have that gift, but like any gift, you must believe it, and accept it, and to do that, you will need to go to God in prayer and confess your sin, and ask for that gift of eternal life like it says in Romans 10:9 and 10."

The parson paused again, looking around at the crowd and added, "Now if you haven't done that, and you still hesitate or wonder, just remember, during this

journey you will see many times when someone, perhaps
that person sitting next to you, will put their life in peril
or danger to keep you or others safe, and this just for a
few days. So let that be a reminder to you that what
Jesus did is forever, and He did it for you. So, we're going
to close with a hymn, and if, after that, anyone has any
questions or would like me to pray with you to receive
that gift, then come to me and we'll get that settled." He
took a deep breath and lifted his hands and said, "Now
let us sing the old hymn, 'Shall We Gather at the River.'"
Everyone joined in and although somewhat out of tune
and timing, they sang:

> Shall we gather at the River?
> Where bright angel feet have trod
> With its crystal tide forever
> flowing by the throne of God
> Yes, we'll gather at the river
> The beautiful, beautiful river
> Gather with the saints at the river
> that flows by the throne of God.

The parson stepped forward, smiled and with arms
outstretched closed with, "Thank you everyone, and the
invitation is always open. If you have any questions, or
just need to talk, come to me at any time. Now, since
we're at the river, maybe we better get to crossin' it, ya'
reckon?" and chuckled as he stepped down and began
packing away the boxes as did everyone else.

The river lay at the base of a long low flat-topped
butte and made a sharp dog-leg bend to the north before
lining out and offering a good crossing with gravel
bottom and shallow water. The wagons had shuttled
back, and the lead wagon was now that of the Fritz

Bondurant family with a matched team of big draft chestnut geldings. The wagon was well-kept and maintained and moved out to the crossing with the high-stepping chestnuts tucking their chins toward their chests and leaning into the harness and collars to lead the way across the muddy water of the North Platte River. It was an easy crossing and the wagons lined out, crossing without incident and the trader's wagons were followed by the big four-up of mules pulling the Thorne wagon.

It was just past mid-day when the river made an "S" bend and turned to the west, but the wagon trail took to the flats well south of the river. Beside the Bridger Trail wagon road was a sign pointing north to a river crossing *Fort Fetterman, 12 miles, 4th U.S. Infantry, Major William E. Dye, Commandant.* Charlie and his shadows had dropped back to the wagons, anticipating a break for a mid-day meal, and Eli nodded to the sign, "That's prob'ly why the Sioux didn't follow us."

"Prob'ly," responded Charlie. "When we stoppin' for noonin'?"

"How 'bout up yonder where them trees offer some shade from that blisterin' sun," nodding to the golden orb that seemed intent on following them. "And since you an' your hunters showed up empty-handed, we'll prob'ly hafta make do with leftover biscuits."

Charlie chuckled, "You might, but I've got an invite to the Proctor wagon. The antelope haunch that young Ted got th' other day is gettin' cooked up with some fresh cornbread by his mama and she an' her hubbin' Jerry, invited me to share!"

Eli grinned. "Suits me. I've had some of her antelope an' cornbread an' I'll stick with my biscuits and jerky, thank you."

Charlie frowned, twisted in his saddle to look back

toward the Proctor wagon and looked again at Eli. "But..."

"Nope, one of the rules of the wagon train is that when you're invited, you accept and be glad of it, otherwise you might spend the rest of the trip eatin' your own cookin'!" Eli chuckled.

Charlie reluctantly reined his buckskin around and started for the Proctor wagon, with a grumble and a scowl at Eli.

———

THE SUMMER ENCAMPMENT of the Brule and Oglala Sioux lay to the west of the long line of hogbacks backed by the painted shoulders of the flat buttes. With almost two hundred lodges, the village lay at the confluence of the Poison Spider Creek and the North Platte River, near the Oregon Trail where the river bent to the south before the confluence with the Sweetwater River that sided the Oregon Trail when it turned to the west and South Pass. The Lakota people were anticipating a good hunt as the migrating bison made their way north. With the treaty of Fort Laramie allowing Red Cloud and his Oglala warriors to dismantle and destroy the soldier forts along the Bozeman Trail and the treaty forbidding settlers and gold hunters to travel that way, the native people were eager for the hunt to provide the meat for the season of green-up and the summer that would follow.

Most of the lodges were of the Brule led by *Siŋté Gleška*, Spotted Tail and *Tȟatȟáŋka Ská*, White Bull, the nephew of the Sioux leader, Sitting Bull, but many were also of the Oglala led by *Tȟašúŋkew Kȟokiphapi*, Young Man Afraid of his Horses and *Sunka Wakan To*, Blue Horse, the brother of the Sioux leader Red Cloud. The leaders and other prominent warriors were gathered in a circle in the central compound of the village as Spotted Tail stood before them. He spoke in the language of the Lakota people, a Siouan language common among the many different bands and understood by all. "Our people hope to have a good hunt of Tatanka. With the treaty signed by our leaders, the forts of the bluecoats are being destroyed and the soldiers leaving. Settlers will no longer travel through the lands of Tatanka, and the herds will not be scattered. We are to decide who will lead our hunting parties into what lands so we will have a good hunt."

A lone warrior jumped to his feet and angrily spoke. "But the White settlers and those that hunt for the gold stone still come. Our young men have just returned after seeing another wagon train of settlers—they do not travel the way of the forts, but are following the river and they say the trader told them they would go west and north to the Wind River west of the Bighorn mountains. They will cross the way of the Tatanka and could ruin our hunt! We must drive them away or destroy them!" The speaker was a young but respected leader of many hunting parties and war parties, Standing Elk.

"Is this the trader that promised rifles for our men?" asked Spotted Tail.

"It is, but they saw the rifles and more destroyed in a blast to keep them from our warriors!" grumbled Standing Elk.

"Are there no others?"

"Our warriors did not know, but left some to follow the wagons and talk to the trader."

"How many wagons and do they have rifles and more?" asked the chief.

"More than three times two hands, and all have rifles and more weapons."

"Then we will wait for word from the scouts. With every day, the wagons come nearer and will make any attack easier. If it is done, it must be complete, and no word taken to the blue coats!" declared the chief to the nods and agreement of all those present.

CHAPTER 12

BATTLE

High above the rolling hills circled many black turkey buzzards. Charlie reined up, watching the carrion eating birds as they caught the updraft winds from the prairie lands dotted with cacti and random piñon and juniper. They were not an unusual sight but with such a large number, there had to be more than the occasional dead animal to attract so many. The birds caught his eye as he crested the tail of a long upthrust ridge at the edge of a mesa that overlooked the lands to the northeast and the distant North Platte River basin. Below him meandered the La Prele Creek that had carved its way from the higher hills on the south to the distant river. He nudged his buckskin to the west end of the mesa where he would have a better overlook of the La Prele valley and the gunsight cut made by the creek through the foothills of the Laramie Mountains.

The crest of the rimrock at the west end of the long mesa stood a little over four hundred feet higher than the valley of the creek and offered Charlie a good promontory for his scan of the terrain below. West and slightly south of his point the long line of foothills showed the cut made by the creek and it was just this side of the cut where the buzzards continued their circling and watching below. With a thorough scan with his binoculars, Charlie decided to go to the area by way of the ridges and hills rather than the creek bottom. Always conscious of the need for cover and high ground, he avoided the inviting green of the valley.

He guessed it to be about two to three miles distant and he chose to go south into the rolling draw between the buttes that held the dry land before making his way west. He would not lose sight of the buzzards and if he did not encounter any trouble, could make it within a quarter hour. The higher hills off his left shoulder still showed patches of the recent spring snow and the breeze that wafted down was cool, prompting Charlie to hunch into his coat and lift his collar against the cold. The shoulder of the hills slid to the flats to expose the red dirt beneath the sage. Charlie stepped down, ground tied his mount, and with rifle in hand, cautiously made his way to the edge of the canyon cut by the creek. The red rock overhung the creek bottom where the shoulders of the hills pushed the creek around a point of red rock cliffs. Charlie dropped to a crouch as he approached the edge, looked over to see what appeared to be four, maybe five or more, bodies with carrion eaters gathered about enjoying the unexpected feast. He spotted the carcasses of two horses and what appeared to be rocker boxes broken and scattered about. These were White men, panning for gold, and attacked unaware with their attention focused on their hoped-for riches.

Charlie returned to his buckskin, stepped aboard and followed the long skirt of red rock and sage as the slope dropped to the creek below. Once at the creek's edge, he turned back upstream and went to the bodies, scattering the ravens, coyotes, badgers, a bobcat, and the few turkey buzzards that remained. The remains of rocker boxes and other gold mining gear lay in the shadow of a natural stone bridge that stretched across the creek, appearing to make an entryway of red and buff-colored rock opening to the distant mountains and the upper reaches of the creek. Clusters of grass and rabbit brush grew atop the natural bridge that also lay in the shadow of a red stone pillar that stood sentinel over the creek bottom.

He looked more closely at the bodies, turned them over and noticed all were scalped, but not in the usual way done by the native warriors, it was a ragged job, not the usual circular cut that took the thickest part of the hair. And the bodies had not been mutilated by the killers, although it was not easy to discern the difference from the gnarled and chewed remains left by the carrion eaters. It was obvious the men had made camp here and had been working for several days, but there was no sign of gold pouches, or other stashes of gold. If they had succeeded, and there was sign enough to prove they had, there would also be sign of their success, but that was gone. Charlie looked about, walked to the overhang where they had made their camp, and there were things like cook pots, gold pans, and more that if this had been the work of natives, those things would have also been taken. There were no weapons, but empty holsters and scabbards, no ammunition, and anything else of interest to outlaws but not natives, was gone. Two of the corpses had their boots removed, something the natives would not take but outlaws in need of better footwear would. Nothing else of any interest to White men remained.

Charlie shook his head, chose to leave the carcasses to the wildlife, and mounted up to return and report to Eli.

As he rode from the area of the natural bridge, he followed the creek, looking to his left at the stained red stone cliffs that rose majestically to give Charlie the sensation of being forced to leave the land of the dead. When he came from the canyon, he pushed his mount from the valley of the creek and took to the high land where he could breathe easier and free from the stench of death. He angled to the northwest and when the sun was reaching its zenith, he spotted the wagons that had stopped for their nooning at the edge of Box Elder Creek. As he neared the wagons, he was greeted by several and when he spotted Eli, he rode to the edge of the trees where Eli sat leaning against a cottonwood, the claybank stallion and grey packhorse drinking at the edge of the creek.

Charlie reined up, leaned on his pommel as he looked at the relaxed Eli who was munching on a leftover biscuit from breakfast and said, "Got'ny more?"

"Sure, get'chur own outta the saddle bag yonder." Nodding to the saddlebags that lay at the base of another cottonwood with the packs from the grey. Charlie stepped down, loosened the girth on his saddle and led the buckskin to the side of the claybank and let him have a drink. Charlie dug in the saddlebags for a couple biscuits and found a seat near Eli. He looked at his friend, "Found somethin' disturbing."

"What's that?"

"A group of gold hunters, five of 'em, killed and left lay."

"Natives?"

"Don't think so," began Charlie, and began explaining what he had found, detailing the missing gear, the condition of the bodies, and more. "So, it looks to be the work of outlaws or marauders, somethin' or someone tryin' to make it look like natives."

"How recent?"

"Yesterday, no earlier. Too much meat left on the bones an' such for it to have been any longer than that."

"What about tracks, horses an' such?"

"They tried to cover 'em, but what I saw was shod horses, and they were headed north from there. Looked to be about six or eight of 'em. They took all the weapons, and if there was any gold, and I think there was, it was gone too. Might try to trade the weapons to the Sioux or..." he shrugged.

"And if it happened yesterday, they could be just about anywhere around here, maybe even be scoutin' out the train," surmised Eli, looking about for any obvious places that would hide that many riders.

"And if they met up with the war party of the Sioux, they could be making a trade with 'em even now. That would put them behind us still, 'cuz I don't think the war party passed us, unless they circled wide around and if so, well..." added Charlie, and shrugged again.

"And we've got another couple days 'fore the Oregon Trail turns south and we keep goin' west into the dry land. The soldiers patrol along the Oregon, but not the Bridger," stated Eli, expressing his thoughts as he looked at Charlie for his input.

"I think our biggest concern is the Sioux war party. They've got mebbe forty warriors, and the outlaws only six to eight. Now, after we push on west, we'll be gettin' into Shoshone country, and mostly they're peaceable and if the outlaws know that, they won't be so anxious to try to do somethin' and make it look like the natives done it," answered Charlie.

"Ummhmm, but either way, we need to have some outriders as well as you scoutin' ahead, and such. I'm thinkin' two outriders on either side, mebbe two behind, and you and another'n ahead. I'll be watchin' the back-trail, you pick someone to go with you out front, and we'll switch off now'n then. What'chu think?" asked Eli.

"Sounds like the best we can do, and we need to make sure everybody else stays alert."

"When we get ready to move out, we'll pick the outriders, then tell the others what we're up against," added Eli.

Chapter 13

Patrol

The thin wisp of smoke that spiraled above the trees near the river told Charlie of the presence of White men, natives would never allow such a giveaway of their presence, unless they were in a large encampment and meals were being prepared by the women. But that would have shown many cookfires, not just one and that coming from a cluster of trees. Charlie nudged his mount nearer the tree line and continued approaching, but keeping behind cover all the while. He motioned his fellow scout, Ezekiel Tabor, the only son of Fred and Audrey Tabor, behind him. Zeke, as he preferred to be called, was only sixteen, but was the size of a mature man nearing six feet tall and a lean hundred seventy pounds, and was a quick learner and a quiet young man, always watchful and careful. He sat quiet and still as he watched Charlie twist and turn, trying to gain a sight of the campers with the cookfire.

Charlie turned, motioned Zeke alongside, and spoke softly, "The trees are too thick to see who's got the cookfire goin', but I'm sure it's not natives. If those are the outlaws that killed the prospectors and ransacked their camp, they'll be trouble, but we can't pass 'em by without knowin'. You get down, move quiet through the woods, try to come up on 'em from the riverbank. I'll approach from here, makin' myself known, and they'll be watchin' me. That way, you can get the drop on 'em from the river. If they're peaceable, you'll know it by what goes on 'tween us an' you can come on in, or I'll call you. Otherwise, don't make yourself known unless it's necessary, got it?"

Zeke nodded, slipped to the ground, his Henry rifle in hand, and after tethering his mount just inside the trees, he started into the thicket. Charlie watched until he was well into the trees, then started toward the camp. As he neared, he heard the sounds of the camp, horses and men moving about, and called out, "Hello the camp! I'm peaceful, can I come in?"

An answering call came. "C'mon in, but keep your hands clear!"

As the trees thinned and the clearing showed, blue uniforms were everywhere. Charlie chuckled as he recognized Union cavalry having their noon break and rest. A tall, lean man stood in the shade of a big cottonwood and nodded as Charlie approached, "Step down and welcome. I'm Lieutenant Coopersmith of C company out of Fetterman." He stepped closer, looked past Charlie, and asked, "You alone?"

Charlie grinned as he stepped to the ground and called out, "Yo Zeke, c'mon in—these are cavalry!" and chuckled as he extended his hand to shake with the lieutenant. "I'm Charlie Two Toes, scoutin' for a wagon train of settlers and gold hunters headin' north on the Bridger Trail. They're back a couple miles or so. Which way you boys goin'?"

"We're headed back to the fort. We've been ridin' guard on a big wagon train headin' west on the Oregon. When they got past the big Sioux camp of Spotted Tail and others, we turned back and sent them on their way," explained the lieutenant. He turned back toward the shade, motioned for Charlie to follow. "You have any trouble?"

Charlie chuckled, shaking his head. "A little. We come on a band of Sioux, mostly young bucks, prob'ly renegades from Red Cloud, they came from the north but near as we could tell they had planned to meet up with a trader that's travelin' with our wagon train, but..." He shrugged and chuckled. "We kinda changed their mind 'bout that. But we also..." continued Charlie and began explaining about his find of the massacred prospectors and his suspicion about it being White men that tried to make it look like the work of natives.

Charlie looked up to see a meek-looking Zeke walking into the camp, leading his bay gelding and looking about at all the blue uniformed men of all ages but when he spotted Charlie, he grinned and nodded and moved toward the shade where Charlie and the lieutenant were standing.

"This is my fellow scout, Zeke," stated Charlie then paused, looked at Zeke and back to the lieutenant. "Zeke, this is Lieutenant Coopersmith."

The two nodded, shook hands and the lieutenant turned his attention back to Charlie. "So your wagons are headed north on the Bridger Trail, that right?"

"That's the plan. You think we're in for trouble?"

"That trail takes you through good buffalo hunting country and there's been a couple big herds movin' north. The Sioux camp we passed had about two hundred lodges and they're huntin', and you're goin' into Shoshone country. Now, Washakie and his people have been peaceful enough, but 'fore that, they were trouble and still could be, young bucks and such. But there's also talk of the Crow comin' over the Big Horns, and some of the Oglala under Red Cloud have been known to hunt this country. All those could lock horns with the Shoshone, they're none too friendly with each other, 'specially during buffalo hunts." The lieutenant paused, stubbed his toe in the dirt, thinking, looked up at Charlie. "You think that bunch that you said were renegades from Red Cloud are still on your trail?"

"Dunno. They were stickin' closer'n ticks for a while, but when we blew up that wagon that had the rifles they were after, they haven't showed themselves. But I'm concerned about the others in that camp yonder, and the outlaws that're raidin' gold diggin's."

"There's not s'posed to be any gold diggings anywhere around here. This is all reservation land and the Shoshone let wagons pass, but they don't hafta let 'em stop and start diggin' for gold." The lieutenant looked at his men who were stretching out in the shade for a little shuteye while the horses grazed and rested. "But if you'd like, we can escort you as far as the crossin' of the North Platte. That's what we're supposed to do, but it's more to make sure you don't try to go north on the Bozeman and into Red Cloud's country."

Charlie chuckled. "Ain't about to do that, had 'nuff fightin' already, down to Washita and such." The lieutenant frowned at the mention of Washita, but did not ask. Charlie continued, "But if you're of a mind, that'd be a help 'cuz if any o' those renegades are up to no good, that might keep 'em away, leastways for a while, less'n they're headed for that camp you passed." Charlie looked at Zeke, "How 'bout you ridin' back to the wagons, tell 'em to stop here for the noonin' and meet the soldier boys."

Zeke nodded, swung back aboard his bay and turned away to start for the wagons. The lieutenant chuckled. "Talkative, ain't he?"

Charlie grinned, nodded, "I like 'em like that."

———

THE LIEUTENANT HAD DIVIDED his troop, keeping half, or about fifty troopers, at the front of the wagons and the other half trailing behind under the leadership of his Master Sergeant. Lieutenant Coopersmith was riding with Eli at the lead, and they spoke of the trail ahead.

The lieutenant explained, "The bridge was built back in '60 by Louis Guinard, he had been a partner with Richard and his brothers who built the first bridge and trading post, but Guinard built a better one and took most of the business away from his partner. He put in a trading post that served the Pony Express and the Stage lines and the army put in a post called Platte Bridge Station, but when they put in Fort Fetterman, they abandoned the post at the bridge. I think the charge now is about $3 per wagon, mebbe less. But the Bridger Trail goes a bit south then almost due west from there while the Oregon follows the river to the south."

"That's what I understood from some I talked with back at Fort Laramie." He looked at the lieutenant, "So, you think Spotted Tail will cause any trouble?"

"Can't tell about them. After the treaty at Fort Laramie with Red Cloud, they're s'posed to be peaceful and for the most part they've kept to it. But you've been around the natives enough to know that you never really know what they're gonna do."

Eli nodded, "For that matter, I've been around enough White men, both in and out of uniform, to know you never really know what they're gonna do either."

The lieutenant frowned, slowly nodding, and mumbled, "Reckon you're right about that."

The troops had accompanied them for the last day and a half and now as they neared the crossing, the sun was lowering in the west and Eli wanted to get the wagons across the river before dark. He and the lieutenant rode ahead to the bridge, saw the trading post was abandoned and there were no toll takers, and the lieutenant doffed his hat, scratched his head, and said, "We were just here three days ago, and he never said anything 'bout leaving."

"Maybe he got gold fever," suggested Eli.

"Well, it's good for you and your wagons, no toll for crossing, so have at it!" declared the lieutenant, waving his arm toward the bridge.

CHAPTER 14

ALONE

The cavalry lined out and crossed back over the bridge to return to Fort Fetterman. After an evening meal and breakfast prepared by the women of the train, the men were sorry to see them go, but oftentimes brief friendships are the best kind. Eli took the lead and with Zeke alongside, they did the scouting while Charlie watched the backtrail. This day was without outriders, the open terrain and low rolling hills offered little cover for any predators, either two-legged or four and Eli believed he could spot any trouble before any outriders and could send Zeke back to warn the wagons.

This was dry country, every footfall of the horses lifted tufts of dust and whenever a rare breeze moved across the flats, it often stirred dust devils to do their twisting dance among the scattered sage and grease-wood. Bunch grass, grama, and Indian grass waved in the breeze and the only sound heard was a muted scream of a falcon and the whistle of the prairie dogs, sometimes called whistle pigs. The trail took the southwest bend and pointed to a gap between a low butte on the southeast and a lone timber covered ridge on the north. The trail rose up the long stretch and crested the saddle to reveal a wide valley below with a meandering creek called Poison Spider Creek showing alkali on the edges but greenery on the banks and shoulders. In the distance low ridges with black timber riding their spines offered the only break in the monotony of the flat buffalo grass-covered plains.

Far to the north, visible only at breaks in the low rolling hills, the Bighorn Mountains were the dividing line between the Bozeman Trail and the Powder River country of the Sioux and Crow, and the Wind River country of the Shoshone, with the Wind River feeding the Bighorn River splitting the Owl Creek mountains with the deep canyon of the Wind River before the confluence with the Bighorn and what some were already calling the Bridger Mountains and taking the Bridger Trail north into Montana. But they would not see the Wind River valley, turning north to cross the saddle between the Bighorn Mountains and the Bridger Mountains, before dropping into the valley of the Bighorn and follow it north. On his left, Eli saw the rolling Rattlesnake Hills and the jagged peaks of the Wind River range that barely marred the horizon in the far distance to the west.

But that was several days away and now they had to cross the dry land that held little promise of water, although spring was the most favorable when the distant mountains still held snow and the spring melt would be carried into the lowlands, offering some respite to early travelers. The dust devils that twisted their way across the two-track trail caught Eli's attention and he spotted a large prairie dog village with many of the little rodents grooming the entrances of their burrows, others grubbing nearby, while several stood on their haunches, watching for predators to warn the rest and allowing them time to disappear into their burrows.

Eli nodded in the direction of the patchwork village that was dotted with low round mounds made by the digging of burrows and marking the land with dusty dots. "That's a prairie dog village, if you ever see one, always ride well around it. That's one of the easiest places to break a horse's leg you'll find in the desert, and where there's prairie dogs, there's coyotes, bobcats and other predators." As he spoke, a shadow whisked overhead, and he looked up to see a low swooping and fast flying peregrine falcon. Within less than a few seconds, the winged predator swooped low, snatched up an unwary rodent just as the watchdog gave his whistle of warning, but it was too late for the one that was now clutched in the talons of the falcon and was lifting high above.

"Wow! That was fast!" declared Zeke, pushing his hat back to get a better look at the falcon and his prey.

"Ummhmm, there's several predatory birds that feed off 'em, owls, falcon, chicken-hawks, eagles, and more."

"Eagles?!" asked an astounded Zeke.

"Ummhmm, I've seen both golden and bald eagles take prairie dogs, jackrabbits, even saw one take a coyote!"

"That had to be sumpin'!"

Eli chuckled, enjoying the eager learning of the young man and remembering the many times of his own first experiences of learning. They were riding on the lee side of a long ridge that showed a series of finger ridges that pointed into the flats toward the trail they followed, and little more than prairie grasses and a few clumps of sage or grease wood dotted the flats. Eli frowned, looking about. He stood in his stirrups and shaded his eyes as he looked toward the long ridge that was about two hundred yards away. He dropped back into the seat of his saddle, twisted toward Zeke and said, "If—" and he felt a blow to his head that knocked him sideways just as he heard the distant report of a rifle. As he started to fall, he grabbed the pommel and clutched the horse with his knees and pointed to the sage, "There!" he yelled and dug his heels to his mount to make the cover.

Zeke was startled, looked at Eli, and immediately obeyed his order and both men slid to the ground just as their mounts slid to a stop behind the tall cluster of sage. Eli grabbed his rifle as he swung down, grabbed the shotgun as he stood beside the claybank, and quickly dropped to the ground behind the cover of the brush. A quick glance showed Zeke had his rifle and was jacking a round into the chamber and asked, "Are you hurt bad?"

"It's a crease, but whoever it is, don't trust 'em. Shoot first." As he spoke, he heard horses approaching and the voices of at least two men as one said, "I know I got him! He's either dead or gonna be!"

"But there's two of 'em and the other'n ain't hit!" growled a second man.

Eli slowly rose, peeking through the thin branches of the sage and spotted four men approaching, using scattered grease wood brush and sage for some cover. He called out, "Stop where you are!"

"Tol' you he ain't dead!" growled one of the attackers.

It was evident these were White men, and Eli guessed

they were the same bunch that had hit the prospectors. Eli glanced to Zeke. "Watch 'em, they'll try coming from both sides," he whispered and saw Zeke nod. Eli felt a stabbing pain in the side of his head and felt blood trickling into his collar. He knew this had to be settled before he passed out from loss of blood.

He turned his attention back to the men and saw movement, "Here they come!" he told Zeke and rose to his feet, lifting the Colt Revolving shotgun. As the first man showed, Eli pulled the trigger on the shotgun and the blast of the big gun shattered the quiet of the prairie and rolled across the flats. The roar of the shotgun was followed by the scream of one of the attackers as he staggered back, dropping his rifle and looking down at his mutilated chest and belly. Blood blossomed over his entire shirt front as he fell to his back, saw the clear blue sky and nothing more.

The rifle of Zeke blasted, and another man stumbled. Eli stepped clear of the sage and brought the shotgun to bear on another man who turned to face him and fired his rifle, but too fast and the bullet ripped through the sage, but the blast from Eli's shotgun tore into the man's torso, knocking him against another man who stumbled and fired his rifle at Zeke, but Zeke's rifle blossomed flame and smoke and caught the man before he hit the ground, driving the bullet through his shoulder and into his neck, making him choke on his own blood.

The thunder of horses told of others that were running away, and Eli stepped clear, looking to see three more riders making dust fly from the heels of their horses as they headed for the high ground of the long ridge. Eli turned to look at the downed men, all but one dead, the fourth one was the first shot by Zeke and the young man stood close by, his rifle pointed at the man as he struggled with his bleeding chest that bubbled blood. With frightened eyes, he looked from Zeke to Eli and said, "Help me," but his words came with bubbles of blood as he choked on his own blood. His eyes wide, but blank, he slowly fell to his back, sightless eyes staring at the cloudless sky.

Zeke looked at Eli, a deep sadness and even fear showing in his eyes. "I never kilt a man before."

"You didn't kill him. He killed himself when they charged at us and tried to kill us. He was dead before he got off his horse."

"But why'd they come after us?"

"Dunno, maybe this is the same bunch Charlie saw, claim jumpers, probably."

"But we don't have a claim, we were just ridin' through!" pleaded Zeke.

"Zeke, you can never tell about people. Those who you think are good people can turn on you in a heartbeat, while others are mean and evil through and through— whatever they do is totally for themselves and they don't care who they hurt, even kill, to get what they want." He paused, looked at the young man and surmised, "These might have been scouts for a bigger group that was lookin' to take the wagons, or at least the traders wagons, maybe more. But now they know we won't be such an easy target. By standing tall like you did today, you've shown the brigands that they might oughta choose another prey. But we might never know why they attacked us, but they did, and all we did was defend ourselves. You've done nothing to be ashamed of, and everything to be confident in, you made the right choice and took the right action."

Zeke turned away, bent over and puked on the sage

and grass and he choked on the bile. Eli went to his mount, lifted the water bag free, and went to the young man. He pulled the cork, poured some water on the back of the young man's head and neck, and handed him the bag, "Rinse out your mouth, and if you need to, take a drink."

CHAPTER 15

WARY

"I'm sorry, Eli," mumbled Zeke as the two men rode their mounts back to the track of the Bridger Trail.

"Sorry? For what?" asked Eli, knowing the young man was fighting the emotions of shame, fear, doubt, and more.

"For...you know," grumbled the young man.

"You have nothing to be sorry for—because you stepped up and did what a good man should, we both are alive. If you had not, it could just as easily have been us laying back there in the dirt." He paused, turned in the seat of his saddle and sat facing Zeke. "Killing a man is never an easy thing and it shouldn't be, but saving the life of another and saving your own life is going to be necessary many more times even before this journey is over. We live in a hard world, and we have to fight to survive, always remember that and don't let that willingness to defend yourself and your friends and family cause you to hesitate in that defense or to feel ashamed for doing what is right." Eli turned back and added, "You took a big step in becoming a man today, and I'm grateful for that."

They had been scouting south of the trail and now returned to the two-track trail that was starting to grow over with new spring growth. With little travel on the road and most settlers and gold hunters taking the Bozeman Trail with the many forts and soldiers to provide safe passage, the Bridger Trail was more difficult and had been seldom used, but now that the Bozeman was closed, they were taking the only other known route north.

The sun was lowering over the low line of the western horizon and dusk would soon bring some relief to the hot day. This was dry land and the only creek beds they crossed were as dry as the skeletons from winter's kill. The horses hung their heads, searching for any green that might yield both food and moisture, but they were disappointed when all that rose was the dust from their own plodding hooves.

The sun tucked itself away and the curtain of dusk covered the land when Eli and Zeke felt their horses quicken their step and as they stood in their stirrups, they could see a line of green ahead. It was a shallow and narrow creek, but it was wet and had cool snowmelt water flowing. They pushed their horses to the bank, stepped down and let the animals drink long and deep, as they put their own faces in the water and drank, scooping handfuls to the back of their necks and to splash on their faces. The two men sat up, grinning and laughing as they looked at the wet faces of each other and Eli said, "We need to head back and get the wagons moving so they can make it here 'fore dark. They need water worse'n we did."

"I can do that if'n you want. It won't be hard to find 'em."

"No, it won't. And it won't be hard for any of that gang of outlaws to find you either. No, we'll go together."

———

Even though it had been a longer day than usual, and it was almost dark as the setting sun sent orange and red reminders of its presence lancing across the sky, the wagons made the creek, circled up, unharnessed, and lined the creek with thirsty animals.

Eli stood back, watching and hollered, "Don't go drinkin' downstream from your horses, that's a good way to get cholera! Go upstream, get fresh water!"

There was some grumbling, a few hard heads scooped water in their hands and drank anyway, but most heeded his words and after letting the animals drink, they went upstream to fill their water buckets and more. Camp was made by the fading light of dusk and the coming of moonlight. The moon was waning to half and the big crescent hung in the western sky, looking like a bowl of porridge he used to shun as a youngster. The memory brought a grin to his face, and he turned back to the wagons to check on everyone and to tell Charlie and the two captains about their run in with the outlaws. Zeke had gone to his wagon and sat leaning against the wheel, watching his mother as she began her preparations for supper. As he leaned back, he picked up a pebble, tossed it at a scampering lizard, and sat back. He heard footsteps nearby and looked up to see Clara Thorne with a bashful smile on her face as she greeted him with "Hi Zeke, heard you been scoutin' with Eli, that right?"

"Yeah, so?"

"Oh nothin', just thought I'd see how ya' been doin'. Can I sit down?"

"Of course," mumbled Zeke. The young man had never been around too many young ladies before and was a tad shy and hesitant, and maybe a little confused, wondering if she had heard about the shooting today.

Clara sat down nearby, using a small box for a seat and with elbows on knees she smiled at Zeke and asked, "So, how'd you like scoutin' with Eli?"

Zeke grinned. "Good and bad. Shows how much I don't know and how much I need to learn, and there's times I just wish I was back here at the wagons and not out there. It can get a little scary or..." he shrugged.

Clara smiled, "When I went out with Charlie and Ted, I was scared we'd run into a bunch of Indians and we'd have a fight, but the only shootin' we done was to shoot some pronghorns. You get to do any huntin'?"

"No, but we saw a few deer and a lot of antelope." He paused, shook his head and looked away, "Then there were the outlaws..." He shrugged, glanced at his ma and back to Clara. He had said nothing to anyone, and wasn't sure if he should, but it was gnawing at his insides, and he felt he had to talk to someone. He stood, motioned for Clara to come with him and they walked together, guided by the moonlight, toward the creek with its cottonwoods and willows, maybe they could find a quiet spot to talk.

ELI HAD BROUGHT the two captains, Nolan Thorne and Mark Ryan, together with Charlie as they gathered around a small cookfire with a dancing coffee pot, and began to relate the happenings of the day. "At first, we thought there were four or 'em, and they took the first shot." He touched the side of his head that he had cleaned up and washed the blood off the crease, "so we knew they weren't friendly. So, we had to take cover, fight back. I killed two, and Zeke killed two, but when the shooting stopped, three others high tailed it outta there, but that's all we saw. For all we know, there coulda been a bunch more back in the hills," He paused, looked at Charlie, "I'm thinkin' they were the same bunch that hit those prospectors and I'm guessin' they had plans on hittin' the wagons. Take out the scouts, me'n Zeke, and they could hit it without warning. They might still be plannin' somethin'."

"So you think we might be in danger?" asked Ryan.

Eli chuckled, "Out here, we're always in danger. We're lucky when we see it first and get prepared. But there's no tellin' what they might be up to and what we might be against. He waved his arm around in a wide arc, "All this is Shoshone country, but they've been peaceful, for the most part, but a bunch like that could get the natives stirred up and they could come against us also."

"So, what'dya think we should do?" asked Thorne, glancing from Eli to Charlie.

"Same thing we've been doin'. Just be careful about everything and everyone. You two," began Eli, nodding to the two captains, "need to spread the word about the possibility of not just natives, but outlaws, and not to be careless about anything or anyone. Just because you see a White man, doesn't mean they're friendly and safe."

"Do we need some outriders, like before?" asked Ryan.

"No, it's still wide open and we could see any threat before it could get too close, but everyone should be wary and careful. If any attackers, native or outlaw, would come at us, it'll be from the front or the rear, most likely, and Charlie and I will be spaced out far enough to give warning. You two, just keep your eyes out to either side of the trail. We've got a few more days before we turn north, but that doesn't mean we'll be out of danger."

"Guards out tonight?" asked Ryan.

"Yeah, two hour shifts, four per shift. You pick 'em," answered Eli. "Now, let's get our supper and get some rest. It's been a long day, but we made good progress. We'll have another long day tomorrow—it's a good distance between water stops."

CHAPTER 16

HUNT

B efore the sun showed its face, the wagons were on the move. Eli was out front, scouting, and his new partner was Ted Proctor, who had scouted and hunted with Charlie and Clara Thorne. The land was showing a pale green as the spring moisture brought life to the grasses and the long trail stretched out beyond the flats and disappeared in the distance. To the right, farther than he could estimate, blue hills lay beneath billowy white clouds, while on the left or south, the Rattlesnake Hills gathered their piñon covered foothills close as if harboring the only trees that showed for many a mile, even though the black timber faded fast the further west they traveled.

By mid-day, the horses and mules began to show the strain of long pulls and powder dry country, and with each low crest, Eli allowed the wagons to stop, give the animals a breather, but pushed them on. He and Ted, although responsible for the scouting, often dropped back to ride beside the lead wagons. Without any obstructions to their view, Eli knew he could see any living thing bigger than a jackrabbit for several miles. Even the grasses that waved in the wind and the sage that was beginning to show buds that would soon bloom purple did little to break the monotony of the flatlands.

Clara was riding her blood sorrel and came alongside Eli, "Mind if I ride with you a spell?" she asked, showing a broad and slightly mischievous smile as she glanced to Ted.

Eli chuckled, knowing the way of young folks and answered, "Sure, but you better keep that rifle handy, we might run into who-knows-what!"

She giggled, slipped the Henry from the scabbard, jacked a round into the chamber and let the hammer down gently, lay the weapon across the bow of her saddle and grinned at Eli, "Oh, I'm ready for who-knows-what!"

Eli chuckled and glanced to Ted who was showing red around his neck and turning away from the others, and said, "Alright then. Maybe you and Ted can get us some fresh meat, but 'bout the only thing around is pronghorn."

"Oh, we know how to get antelope, don't we Ted?" She grinned and gave Ted a sideways glance.

Early afternoon saw Eli and the two youngsters standing beside their mounts, waiting for the wagons as they neared a crossing of a sandy-bottomed dry wash. This was Wallace Creek that fed the South Fork of the Powder River, but it was almost dry now. Although the sandy draw showed sign of recent moisture, it appeared as nothing but sand and gravel, it was not unusual for dry gulches to swallow up runoff creeks and carry the moisture underground before surfacing again some distance away. Eli waved down the lead wagon, driven today by Fritz Bondurant, "Fritz, when you approach the bottom, slap your animals with the reins and take the sand as quick as you can, the other side of the wash will be a bit of a pull, but it's not far to the flats up top. Make room for the others and pull off to the side, we'll have a bit of a break for noonin' but there's no water to be had. You'll hafta use what'chu got for your animals, and we won't hit water till sometime tomorrow, so be sparing, and pass the word to others."

"Understood!" nodded Fritz and started his animals down the slight slope, one foot on the brake lever, the other on the footboard and his eyes on the trail.

The wagon creaked, groaned, and squealed, but as he neared the bottom, Fritz let off the brake, slapped the horses, and took the sandy bottom quickly and started up the other side without slowing. He set the example for the others and Eli watched as each wagon made the crossing. It wasn't until the freighters, heavier than the others but drawn by a four up of mules, that the wagons bogged down in the sand. Eli directed Catlin, "Get that spare team harnessed and up front. You'll need to hook on and pull the heavy wagons outta the sand."

"Yeah, an' if'n you didn't make us ride the rear, we coulda crossed without any trouble!" grumbled Catlin.

Eli shook his head. "So, you'd rather a family and their wagon or wagons would bog down instead of yours?"

Catlin turned away, grumbling and growling, but did as instructed and was soon leading the spare team of harnessed mules down the hillside beside the trail and began hooking them to the stuck wagon and team. Once the extra team was added, Catlin hollered at the teamsters to help each other out and use the levers and more to free up the bogged wagon. Once the wagon was free and started up the trail, Catlin scouted out the creek bottom, picked out a spot where he thought his wagons could cross and cut back to the trail and cut away from the trail to make his crossing with the heavy wagons.

When all the wagons were gathered up top, Eli rode among them, warning them about the lack of water, and added, "If we're careful and sparing on the water, we'll make water at Keg Spring, but it ain't much, just enough to fill your barrels and keep you going until the next stop."

He looked at the somber faces of the people, and added, "But in a few days, after we turn north, we'll come to the Bighorn River, and we'll have all the water we need. You ladies could even do some wash and some of you men could use a bath!" He grinned as he said it and the remark brought a few smiles and laughter which lightened things a little. "So, let's get to movin', we've a long way to go yet today!"

It was a dry run for the next two days, but as dusk began to settle over the land, the horses' heads perked up, nostrils flared, and their step quickened. The road turned north at Needles Eye Butte and took to the shoulders well north of Poison Creek, but fresh water was not to be found, even when they crossed Alkali Creek, they avoided the water and kept moving, hopeful of fresh water ahead. Low willows crowded the banks, but at Eli's word, the wagons stayed clear of the meandering shallow creek. It was muddy water with a bitter stench that trickled over the rocks and everyone's spirits sagged. Parched throats longed for fresh water and the people and horses and mules drank sparingly of their rationed portions carefully measured out to keep the animals sound.

Eli noticed Parson Spencer working his way along the line, encouraging each one, giving God the glory for bringing the wagons safely thus far and arranging an impromptu prayer and praise meeting after supper. Eli chuckled, remembering the off-key voices of most of the men and several of the women, but they did not lack for enthusiasm.

Eli saw Clara talking with Zeke and he motioned them both over and asked, "You think you two would like to go with me to see if we can get some fresh meat? We might find some deer comin' to water a little further upstream."

Zeke grinned, looked at Clara and when she smiled and nodded, he turned to Eli, "Yessir, we'd like that. I'll go get our horses and be right back!"

Eli grinned and nodded, and turned back to Rusty and the grey, having stripped the gear off both and had been rubbing them down with some dry grass, and began rigging them up again. The horses had been refreshed with the relief from their burdens, a roll in the dirt, and the rub down and were eager to be on the go again. When Zeke returned with their horses, Clara was grinning as she led her sorrel and Zeke had his bay. Neither had been riding most of the afternoon, but rode and walked with their families as did most of the others.

Eli told Charlie where they were going and at his nod, he led the other two hunters from the wagons, heading upstream on Alkali Creek. They came to the confluence of another smaller creek, kept to the north bank and continued toward the deeper draws and rolling hills with deep cut ravines that held more piñon and scattered willows and skeleton cottonwood. They were about fifteen minutes away from the wagons when Eli reined up, pointed to a cluster of cottonwoods that sided the little creek, and slowly stepped down, motioning the two young hunters to do the same.

With rifles in hand, the two came to the side of Eli,

and Eli pointed through the cottonwoods, "There's three or four deer yonder. From what I saw, there's at least one young buck, maybe two." He pointed out the way for the two to go, separating them in the routes, and added, "Zeke, you'll be in place before Clara, but wait till she takes the first shot. You choose your target as the one closest to you, and you do the same, Clara. I'll stay here with the horses, now stay low and stay quiet."

He watched as the two eager hunters started into the edge of the trees. They moved quietly and Eli guessed they would soon be in position, but neither shot, and he saw and heard the deer scamper away. Within moments, the two came back, still in a crouch and moving quietly. Clara came close and said, "We couldn't shoot. Just beyond the creek, there's a camp that looks like natives."

"How many?" asked Eli as Zeke came near.

"Hard to say, at least twenty, maybe more. One of 'em took the little buck with an arrow," answered Zeke, glancing to Clara and back to Eli.

"You did right. Let's see if we can get away without being seen." They swung aboard their mounts, reined them around and Eli took the lead to lead them back to the wagons.

Chapter 17

Buffalo

It was a musky, even dusty, smell, but it was a recognizable odor known to those that have traveled the plains and known the ways of the wilderness. It was distinguishable by those that had known it and experienced it firsthand, and there was a difference that most would think would be recognizable by only those of the canine or similar species, but the distinctive and pungent smell of the bison as it traveled in vast herds took over the very breeze that carried it toward those that would be hunters or travelers. Eli immediately recognized the musky scent of the buffalo or as the Sioux called them, the *tatanka*, and knew it was a large herd that carried the stench that attracted predators and the cowbirds that rode their backs. It also explained the presence of the hunting party of Shoshone. This was the land of the Snake people and the hunting grounds of their respected chief, Washakie.

He led the way to the wagons and explained to the two disappointed hunters what was carrying the odor.

"Buffalo?" asked Carla, hope showing in her eyes. "Can we go after them in the morning?"

"Only if you want to fight that hunting party of Shoshone for them, and if you did, I think you'd lose. The buffalo are what supports the natives of the plains. They use every part of the animal, from the hide and horns to the marrow of the bones. Their dinner plates are often the scapula bones, their homes are made from the hides, their winter clothes are from the pelts, the glue that is used to seal the seams comes from the hooves, the thread that sews the seams from the sinew, and more. No, we'll not fight them for the meat of a few bison, we will instead leave the herd to them and go our way, hopefully in peace."

They rode into the wagon circle by the light of the moon, were greeted by all but Eli nodded to the captains and Charlie and pulled them aside. When they gathered outside the circle, Eli explained, "We about run into a sizable party of Shoshone, and I know they're mostly friendly, but I didn't want to take any chances. There's a big herd of bison on the move into the Wind River Basin and we'll be pullin' out early. We'll be headin' north into the hills yonder and if we're lucky we might run into some buffalo, maybe some elk, and plenty deer. So, try to keep the folks in line and we'll get outta here without a fight."

"Mebbe so, but some buffler steak would sure taste almighty good 'bout now," declared Mark Ryan who was standing beside Trey Sheridan, another of the men bound for the gold fields and was grinning broadly, "You're right 'bout that, but it's kinda hard to eat steak with an arrow sticking through your neck!"

The other men chuckled, all agreeing with Sheridan's assessment of the possibilities.

———

It was first light when the wagons began to move. The long shadows of early morning stretched before them, but they soon turned north just as the sun made itself known and began to warm their right shoulders and stretch their shadows into the bottom of the low swale that pointed them north toward a distant low saddle that lay between far-away flat-top mesas whose shoulders had been carved in years gone by with spring runoffs that washed the clay soil down into the flats. Late morning saw the wagons pushing across the shallow Sand Creek and Badwater Creek, the trickle of muddy water was tempting but the alkali banks and the smell of bad water kept the animals from dipping their noses as they crossed the alkali bottom land to take to the dry hills beyond. They kept on the move with the promise of water just ahead and by noonin' time, they came to the confluence of two creeks, one from the grassy bottomed valley to the north and the other from a deeper gully to the northeast that cut between adobe and red clay hills.

The wagons stretched out along the creek, giving the animals water and graze while the folks had their breakfast leftovers for their noon meal, but Eli had them back on the trail in short order and they stayed on the east side of the creek, going north before crossing a smaller feeder creek and with their sights on the shadowed shoulder of a high rimrock butte, they kept pushing. The trail offered good road, occasional patches of grass for the eager animals to snatch as they passed, and rising hills on either side. To the west rose the tallest of the mountains that stood well over two thousand feet higher and showed broad pine covered shoulders while other timbered hills rose to the north and tempted those thinking of fresh meat. Eli knew their route would take them between the two mountain ranges and this was the land where he hoped to find some elk and maybe a few wandering buffalo. It had been a long day and still they pushed on with the trail taking them into the face of red bluffs that rose high above the trail and topped out with flat-topped buttes, but when he called for the stop, everyone was relieved and anxious for some rest, animals included. With a day of rest declared, the people set about mending harness, greasing hubs, making minor repairs and the women set to making a bigger meal than usual.

Eli had set out alone, wanting to go to the higher timber covered mountains to the west and look for some elk. With the grey packhorse behind, he took to the mountains at first light, looking forward to the time of solitude. He had stopped when well away from the wagons to spend his usual time in prayer, sitting atop a rock outcropping and watching the sun come up as he read and prayed, which set the tone for the day.

As he gave Rusty his head, they started following a dim game trail that led from the little trickle of a creek that was hidden in the willows, and took them higher up the shoulders of the mountains and into the kind of country that Eli had often thought of as *my kind of country*. He was confident in Rusty and as the big stallion easily picked his way on the narrow, pine needled covered trail, Eli let his mind wander down the halls of contemplation.

He grinned to himself as he began to picture the memories of the women he had known in his time since the death of his wife. Although he and Margaret had a marriage of respect and convenience and the result of a promise he made to a dying friend and her husband, he had provided for her and been a husband to her, as much as his military career and the war would allow, it was not a marriage of deep love. He had never known that type of relationship with any woman, but his extended search for his stepsons, again as the result of a promise made to his dying wife, had led him across the country and brought other women into his realm of friendship. He had often thought of having a wife and children of his own, especially during the tumultuous times of the war when life was cheap and short, but life had never allowed him to have that dream fulfilled.

He grinned to himself as he considered some of the women he had met in recent times. There was Constance Wellington, the beauty on the riverboat who was a savvy investor and businesswoman, unusual for the time, and she had made it known to Eli that she would enjoy making a life with him, but she would not be willing to stay in the west, preferring the life of the city which definitely was not for Eli.

And there was the Blackfoot or Piikani woman, Morning Dove, the sister of the wife of Chief Running Rabbit, the respected leader of the Blackfoot in Montana. She wanted Eli to stay with them in their village and make a life with her, even after he left and met up with her some time later, her eagerness to be his woman was made clear, but he was still intent on his search for his stepsons and could not stay with her. He wondered if she was still alone, for just the thought of her brought a smile to his face and made him take a deep breath.

But that breath also brought with it the unmistakable scent of elk! He reined Rusty to a stop, stood in his stirrups and searched through the trees, watching for movement, but the fir and spruce were thick and branches low, making it difficult to see, but he heard the movement of many and the smell of elk was strong. Rusty and

Grey stood still, heads lifted, ears pricked and nostrils flaring as they too looked uphill and into the trees.

Eli nudged Rusty into the trees, picking his own way to move parallel with the movement of the herd. The terrain across the face of the mountain was one of ridges and gullies, but the dim trail that led them through the thicker trees, moved slightly uphill and across the head of a long draw. He could still hear the movement of the animals and could tell there were many, but at this time of year, most of the bulls were separate from the cows and newborn calves. He did not want to take a cow with a calf, preferring to take a young bull or two.

He saw the dark brown legs moving through the trees and as he leaned to look around a big spruce, he saw the animals move into a broad open park with deep grass and a trickle of a snow melt creek that meandered through the sloping park. The herd slowed, spread out, and began to pick their individual feeding spot.

Eli drew Rusty to a stop, spotting a small clearing with grass and the same trickle of a creek, and moved the claybank into the clearing that was hidden from the big park of the elk, and with the stallion and the grey pack-horse picketed, he slipped the big Spencer from the scabbard and began his stealthy approach to the park. Moving in a crouch, and picking his steps on the pine needle covered forest floor, keeping a big spruce between him and the herd. As he neared, he dropped to his knees, looking under the low branches of the big spruce and searched the herd for his target. As he suspected, this was a gang of bulls, all with at least small stubs of velvet covered spikes showing, some already showing branched antlers, still in the velvet, and he knew those would become the herd bulls of their own harem, but that would be later in the summer, early fall.

He spotted a bull with beginning antlers that showed their first fork and thick with velvet, a body that was well filled out and would offer good meat. He slowly and as quietly as possible began drawing the hammer of the Spencer back, heard the scolding chatter of a squirrel and used the sound to mask the clicking of cocking the hammer. As he readied, he also picked a second target, he sat down, drew up his knees and with elbows on knees, he lined up his sight on the young bull. But just as he was ready to drop the hammer, the wind kicked up and several of the bulls, including his target lifted their heads at the squeal of a dead snag rubbing against another and the breaking of a branch. They twitched their muscles at their shoulder, and leaned as if ready to bolt, but Eli squeezed off his shot and the big Spencer roared, bucked, spat fire, smoke and lead, and before the targeted bull could spring away, the bullet bore into his neck, breaking the neck bone and felling the big bull.

The rest of the herd moved as if attached at the hip and within seconds the thundering herd broke through the trees and disappeared. Eli stood, returned to his horses and slipped the Spencer back into the scabbard, and led the horses into the clearing to start the butchering. He chuckled to himself as he thought of the good tasting meat, and shook his head at the thought of the hard work of butchering. But when he broke into the clearing, he stopped, frowning, as he saw a buckskin clad woman already beginning the work of field dressing the animal. She looked up at Eli, a somber expression on her gaunt face and waited for him to speak or move. Eli took a step closer and asked, "Why are you working on my kill?"

She looked from him to the elk and answered, "I have been following the herd for two days. I was getting close and would make a kill, but you shot first and they fled. I was too tired to continue and thought we could share."

Eli was surprised at the clarity of her speech, her English was more fluent and proper than many Whites, and he knew she had to have had some teaching, perhaps in a White school. "Do you have family waiting?" asked Eli, moving closer and turning to picket his horses. He glanced over his shoulder at the woman who returned to her work.

"My father, mother, and sister are back at my lodge."

"Are you with a village?"

"No, my father and mother are old and left the village to join our ancestors, but my sister and I chose to go with them."

"Then we will share," responded Eli, watching the skill with which the woman worked. She had a trade knife, and used it quickly and efficiently. He looked at her and grinned to himself as he went to the tail of the elk, spread the big legs and holding them apart with his feet, he bent down to begin splitting the big bull from tail to chin.

She was an exceptionally pretty woman, her buckskin tunic covered her leggings, both adorned with simple yet colorful beadwork, fringed at the seams, and fitted very well to her perfectly formed figure. He guessed her age to be mid to late twenties, and noticed her dark eyes did not miss any movement of his and she had also looked him over. *Hmmm, this might be one of the most interesting and rewarding hunts I've ever had,* he thought as he continued his work. They worked well together, both knowing what the other was doing and complementing the work on their portion of the carcass as well.

Eli looked up at the woman, "Your lodge far?"

"Not far."

"Do you have a horse to carry the meat?"

She grinned, nodded to the edge of the clearing where he could see into the edge of the trees and see an appaloosa with a blanketed saddle aboard. Eli nodded, continued his work, yet stole a glance at her as she moved quickly.

Eli said, "My name is Eli, and yours?"

"I am called *Chosro*, Bluebird."

Chapter 18

Bluebird

They were on the east face of Copper Mountain when they loaded the hide wrapped meat aboard the horses. Eli asked, "How far to your lodge?"

"Not far, I followed the herd from beyond the mountains"—nodding to the peak of Copper Mountain— "they came around that side"—nodding to the south face of the big mountain which was more than just one tall peak, but a cluster of tall buttes and hills, covered with pines, spruce and aspen—"but the timber is sparce and I could not get close enough for a good kill shot with my bow. Our lodge is on the far side of the peak"—nodding to the north face.

Eli glanced to the sun, knowing it was early morning yet and the wagons would not be moving until the following day. He had offered to help her haul the meat to her lodge and she readily accepted, with a coy smile as she gathered the deboned meat into a big bundle of hide. She had deftly cut the hide into quarters, leaving large enough portions of hide to be cured into usable leather, while making bundles for the meat. Two were placed on the grey, one each on Eli's claybank and Bluebird's appaloosa. The stallion had crowded closer to the appaloosa mare and was showing his interest while the mare was not too resistant nor interested in his overtures.

Both Eli and Bluebird laughed at the antics of the horses and Eli said, "We'll have to keep them separated if we expect to get the meat to your lodge." Bluebird dropped her eyes and let a quiet giggle escape as she glanced up at Eli and nodded.

It was just over an hour when Bluebird pointed ahead through the trees and said, "Our lodge is there." Through the trees, Eli could see the painted hide lodge and smelled the smoke from the cookfire as they broke from the trees to see an old man, heavy grey hair and wrinkled face, leaning back against a willow branch backrest, and an old woman sitting atop a rock beside a cookfire with a heavy pot hanging from a metal tripod, a luxury few women enjoyed. They both frowned as they looked at Bluebird leading the way and a White man behind her.

Bluebird held her hand up to greet her parents, looked around for her younger sister but not seeing her, asked, "Where is Squirrel?" but she spoke in the tongue of the Shoshone, a tongue familiar to Eli although he was not fluent.

The woman responded. "Gathering berries, if there are any."

Bluebird glanced to her father who appeared to be snoozing, turned back to motion Eli forward and as he nudged Rusty forward. "This is Eli, he helped me with the elk." She turned toward her people, back to Eli and said, "This is my mother, Rabbit Tail and my father, *Chochoco*, Has No Horse."

Eli glanced to Bluebird, frowning, remembering during his time at Fort Laramie he had heard of Chief Washakie of the Shoshone and his cousin, Chochoco. He looked back to the old man, thinking he was too old to be the cousin of Washakie, but he did not ask. Bluebird stepped down, motioned for Eli to do the same and untied the bundle of meat from her blanketed saddle, and carried it to the edge of the cookfire and spoke softly to her mother. Eli also removed the bundle behind his saddle and placed it beside that of Bluebird's. She looked up at Eli, frowning, "But that is yours," she began, but Eli held up his hand, and motioned to the bundle and her mother, and with sign language, spoke, "It is yours for your family."

He turned away, started to his horse, and was stopped when Bluebird spoke, "You must stay and eat with my family."

He looked at Bluebird, glanced to her mother and her snoozing father, nodded, and led the horses back to the edge of the trees to picket them and strip them of their gear to give them a bit of a rest and let them graze and water. When he had begun stripping them, Bluebird came near and spoke softly. "My mother and father are near the end of their time, and they want us to return to the village of my people. I do not want to leave them, but it is the way of my people."

"I understand. I know it must be hard, but you have provided well for them. Do you have someone special in your village?" asked Eli, trying to appear casual in his question.

"No, I did have a man that wanted me for his mate, but..." she paused. "I did not want to leave them," she finished, nodding to her parents. As they spoke, Eli saw a younger woman come from the far side of the lodge, stop and look at them and slowly come nearer. Bluebird smiled, motioned her close, "This is my sister, *Nanawu*, Little Striped Squirrel. She was given the name of my grandmother." The girl appeared to be in her late teens, mature, but shy as she stayed slightly behind her sister Bluebird, but Bluebird reached behind to pull her close. "*Nanawu*, this is Eli, my friend. He helped me get the elk." Squirrel nodded, dropped her eyes and stepped back, whispered to Bluebird and received and smile and a nod as the girl turned away to return to the lodge.

With the animals picketed and fresh meat added to the cooking pot, Bluebird motioned for Eli to join her, and they walked from the camp to a trail in the edge of the trees. Their camp was on a shoulder and the trail led to a promontory that offered a long view of the valley below and Bluebird pointed, "Your wagons are there," prompting Eli to look and with a squint and shading his eyes, he could see the white bonneted wagons in the circle near the small stream.

He turned to look at her. "How did you know I was with the wagons?"

"One man has no need of a whole elk. I knew you were getting meat for others," she smiled. "That is why I will go with you to get more meat for your people." She paused, sat down on a lichen covered boulder, leaned back and looked at Eli, "You go far?"

"We are going to the gold fields in Montana territory. We will travel for some time."

"Have you been that way before?"

"No, but I've talked to several who have, and I'm good at following a trail."

"There are Crow, Sioux, and Cheyenne, even some

Blackfoot that might not be friendly. They may see you as an enemy." She leaned back on her elbows, looked sidelong at Eli and almost as an afterthought added, "I could guide you and keep you from their lands."

Eli tried to remain somber, but was smiling inside and kept himself from chuckling, "You'd do that?"

"Of course, you have shown me kindness, I should do the same."

"What about your sister?"

"She could come also; she is a good cook. Perhaps some young man of your people would like to sample her cooking," she giggled.

"But what about after we get to the gold fields, then what would you do?"

"The land of my people goes to the Three Forks, we have others near there," she appeared almost saddened by his question.

Eli looked away, knowing he could not do as some early trappers and traders were known to do and take a woman as a wife for a season then leave her behind. Although he had been pondering his future and what he would do, and much of his thinking had been about taking a wife, this was a little too sudden. Although she was a beauty, and he was taken with her. He looked down the hillsides to the distant valley and the wagons below, wondering what the people of the wagons would think. He would have to make proper arrangements for the girls to be with a family, although Bluebird would ride with him during the day, but they could not...he shook his head at the thought. He turned to look at her, "Let me think about it. We had not planned on such an arrangement, and you would have to be with another family, but..." He shrugged.

Squirrel came from the trees and said, "Mother says to come eat."

———

AFTER THE MEAL, Eli rigged his horses, swung aboard and was surprised to see Bluebird sitting on her appaloosa waiting. He chuckled, "Goin' somewhere?"

"You helped me and shared the elk. You said you were going after another. I will go with you and help you." It was a statement that allowed no argument, for Eli knew to refuse the offer would be a great insult to her and her people. He breathed a deep sigh, grinned, nodded and reined the claybank stallion around with the grey behind and started back to the game trail. He had said his goodbyes and thanks to her family, and rode in a contemplative mood, wondering just what would be the right thing to do. He was not looking for a wife, but he had been considering the possibilities. He turned to look at her as she casually sat her appaloosa riding behind the grey, looked back to the trail and came into the open park where they had taken the first bull. The herd had scattered, but he spotted some of the larger prints and knew they would be the herd bulls or the larger of the bunch and chose to follow those. He pointed to the break in the trees, nudged the claybank toward the track and entered the shaded woods, anticipating catching up with the other bulls soon, hopefully before dusk.

Chapter 19

Decision

Eli was thinking about an older couple on the wagon train, Max McCoy and his wife, Violet. Good people that were going to Montana to homestead and make their life on a farm that would raise crops to feed the miners. They were childless and Violet had confided in Eli one time after their church service with pastor Spencer, that they had twin girls who died shortly after birth and she could no longer have children, but she wished they could have a family and asked Eli to pray for them. Bluebird and Squirrel were not children, but they were sisters and Squirrel was still young, midteens probably, but Bluebird was older and not a child in any respect. He grinned at that thought, *She certainly is not a child!*

The trees thinned and the trail widened. It was evident many of the bulls had regrouped and were moving together, probably to a previously used grazing area. They followed the trail that led them down into a wide draw, up the far side and to the crest of a ridge, but Eli reined up before the crest, motioned to Bluebird to wait and he stepped down, ground tied the claybank and in a crouch, moved quietly to the crest to look on the far side. He had noticed the smell and thought they were close, and he was right, just over the crest the terrain leveled out into a wide grassy park nestled in a vale between two long ridges and protected with tall timber on three sides.

He looked back to Bluebird, nodded, and pointed over the ridge, grinning. She motioned to him, to herself, and asked with sign if he wanted her to come, but he shook his head, turned back to look at the herd and picked his target. A bull about the same size as the one already taken, grazing with head down, and angled slightly away and downhill. He slowly brought the Spencer up, brought it to full cock, and lined up the sights to just behind the front leg, low on the chest. He took a breath, let a little out and slowly squeezed the trigger. The big Spencer barked with a roar that echoed across the vale, spitting fire, smoke and lead, and the slug flew true, driving the bull to his knees and dropping him to his side. The bull's hind legs kicked once, and he lay still, but the rest of the herd lunged together into the trees and quickly disappeared. Eli turned to see Bluebird already coming up the hill, leading his claybank and the grey. He stood, looked at the downed bull and back to Bluebird as she came alongside and handed him the reins to his stallion.

She could see into the park from where she sat and saw the downed bull. "You have done well. You are a good hunter."

Eli chuckled, knowing that quality was one held in high regard by native women as they considered possible mates. Any man must be a good hunter, provider, and warrior, and the smile on her face was one of approval.

Eli shook his head. *What am I thinking? What am I getting myself into—trouble more'n likely.*

They made short work of field-dressing the elk, packed the bundles on the horses and with the heavy loads, started for the wagon train. They had dropped from the flanks of the timbered hills and were in the flats, the wagon train in view and Eli began to explain, "We'll go to the wagons, and have one or two of the men divide the meat among the different families, then I'll go with you back to your lodge."

"You do not want me to guide for you?" asked Bluebird, frowning as she looked at Eli.

"I'll need to talk to some of the people. If we decide to have you guide, we'll need a place or family for you to stay with, you know, to sleep at their wagon. One of the couples, probably the wagon where we'll stop, might be a good couple for you to stay with at night, and maybe your sister also."

Bluebird frowned. "You do not want me to stay with you?"

Eli grinned, cocked his head to the side. "That's not how it's done with these people. If we were to stay together, we would need to be married, you know, joined as a couple."

Bluebird smiled coyly. "That would be good. You are a good hunter and I think you are a good man. Would you not like to be joined with me?"

Eli dropped his head, trying to think this out and explain it so she would understand and not be offended or hurt. "We need to spend some time getting to know one another. After you get to know me better, you might not like the idea of being joined with me."

"I have never thought this way before," mumbled Bluebird, looking away.

As they came to the wagons, Eli was quick to spot the wagon of the McCoy couple and rode directly toward the space between the McCoy's and the Tabor wagon. As they entered the circle, they were greeted by many that came near and Eli stepped down, noticing the looks both he and Bluebird received as they began unloading the bundles of meat. Eli turned to Max McCoy and asked, "Mr. McCoy, would you be so kind as to begin dividing up the meat for the folks? Make sure everyone gets a fair share. That was hard to come by for Bluebird and me," nodding to Bluebird who was struggling with a large bundle from the packsaddle aboard the grey.

Eli helped her and said, "Bluebird"—nodded toward Violet McCoy—"this is Violet McCoy. How 'bout you helping her with her meat?"

Bluebird nodded, smiled, turned to Mrs. McCoy, extended her hand, "Pleased to meet you, Mrs. McCoy. How may I help you?"

"And I'm happy to meet you too, Bluebird. Join me at the table, if you would please."

Eli chuckled, knowing the way of women, especially lonely women, and knew that Bluebird would be questioned endlessly, but he thought it would be good for the two to become acquainted before he asked about Bluebird and possibly Squirrel, staying with them. He stepped beside Max and opened another bundle, slipped his Bowie knife from the sheath at his back and began cutting off some meat to pass to one of the families. While they worked, Max asked, "Where'd you find her?" nodding to the table where Bluebird and Violet were working and getting acquainted.

"Well, I had been stalking a herd of elk, they stopped, I got down, shot one, went to retrieve my horses and when I came back, she was already skinning the elk.

Come to find out, she had been after them for a day or two and I spoiled her hunt, so we agreed to share. Went back with her to take the meat to her family, found out her parents had left the village to prepare to meet their ancestors," and paused as he noticed the frown on Max's face. He continued to explain. "When the elders of the plains Indian tribes grow old and near death, they usually leave the village, go off by themselves to die. But the girls, Bluebird and her younger sister, over the objections of their parents, chose to go with them."

Eli worked for a while in silence until Max asked, "But if the old ones leave to die, what happens to the young ones?"

"They usually stay until near the end, help them find food and such, then leave to allow the old ones to die in peace and solitude." Eli glanced to see the frown on Max's face, but he continued dividing the meat bundles, obviously thinking about what he had learned.

"Bluebird has offered to help guide our wagons north. It's a trail she knows, and she can speak the tongues of the different native people we might encounter—the Sioux, Cheyenne, Crow, and even Blackfoot."

"Are you goin' to take her on?" asked Max, looking to Eli.

"Dunno. Need to talk to the captains, think on it, but..."

"But you can't have her sleepin' with you, these folks wouldn't stand for it!" declared Max.

"Nor would I. I don't believe it right for unmarried folks to be together like that. If she and her sister would accompany us, they would need to camp separately or be with someone in the train."

Max glanced to Eli, frowned, and turned his attention back to his meat cutting.

———

Violet had brought Bluebird to their makeshift table where she lay out their portion of meat, glanced to Bluebird and asked, "Who are your people, Bluebird?"

Bluebird dropped her gaze. "We are called the Eastern Shoshone, led by the great chief, Washakie. Our band was the *Tukkutikka*."

"And how did you find Eli?" he nodded toward the two men with their backs to them.

Bluebird smiled. "He shot an elk I had been following to take for my family. We agreed to share, and he helped me take it back to my lodge."

"To your village?"

"No. My father and mother are old and had left the village to make their journey to our ancestors. My sister and I went with them to provide for them before they took that journey."

"And have they taken that journey?"

"No, my sister is still with them, but we will leave soon, now that they have meat and more until that time."

The women worked in silence for a while until Violet spoke. "My grandmother was Cherokee, and my grandfather's mother was also. I have never seen any of my people."

"I do not know the Cherokee," responded Bluebird.

"They are a people that lived far to the east, where the sun rises. They were forced from their land in the 1830's and made to travel the Trail of Tears where many died before crossing the great river called the Mississippi. Those that remain are in what they now call Indian Territory. They were a great people."

"But you are not with them?"

"No, my husband and I are going north to Montana territory to have a farm and raise crops to feed the many people that hunt for gold."

"You do not have children?"

"No, even though we tried. I had twin girls who died as babies and cannot have more." Violet worked in silence for a few moments, remembering, then looked at Bluebird. "Do you not have a mate?"

"No, I have never been joined. There were some that tried to buy me from my father, but he would not make me go to any man. But if we return to the village, the elders could make us join with one that would provide for us and more. But I believe I could provide for me and my sister. I am a good hunter and have proven myself as a warrior." Bluebird spoke with determination and resolve, her knife working on the meat as her emotions rose.

Violet watched the woman, let a grin split her face as she watched Bluebird work at the meat. "Do you like Eli?" she asked, having noticed the way Bluebird kept Eli within her sight.

"He is a good man. He is a good hunter, and he works for his people."

"But do you *like* him, you know, as a mate?" asked Violet.

"He says we must get to know each other before that is to be considered, but I believe I know all I need to know. I have offered to guide the wagons to the Three Forks, where the trail turns to where those that hunt the yellow stone want to live."

Violet smiled, lifting her eyebrows in a moment of revelation, "But he won't let you come because he will not let you camp with him, is that right?"

Bluebird turned to look at Violet, cocked her head to the side and answered, "Why is that?"

Violet smiled, turned to the men and walked over to stand beside Eli, touched him on the elbow and said, "If you decide to have Bluebird guide for us, she and her sister will stay with us at our wagon. We would love to have them"— she glanced to her grinning husband, "wouldn't we, Max?"

Max chuckled, nodded, and turned back to the disbursing of the meat. He glanced at a perplexed Eli and said, "When a woman makes up her mind, it's best just to nod and agree."

CHAPTER 20

CREEKSIDE

The trail bent to the north, passed a lonesome butte that rose off their left shoulder, and pushed into a draw with a trickle of a willow-lined creek and high buttes shouldering the draw. With rust-red and pale dun streaks that appeared as layers of clay soil stacked one atop the other, the dry buttes showed themselves to be long ridges pointing the way north for the travelers on the Bridger Trail. By late morning and under a clear azure sky, the little trickle fed into another creek where they stopped for the nooning.

When Charlie came in from his scout, he joined Eli and Bluebird at their fire under the cottonwoods. He grinned at Eli, glanced to Bluebird who was pouring the men some hot coffee in the tin cups, and he said, "Nice to have a woman about, don'tchu think?"

"Don't get too used to it, she didn't sign on to be a cook, but a guide," responded Eli, nodding to Bluebird as she brought the cups to the men. "Ain't that right, Bluebird?"

The woman smiled and nodded, "As you say, Eli." She

seated herself nearby, holding her own cup out as she sat down.

Charlie looked at Bluebird. "You know the name of this creek?"

"That is called Kirby Creek, my people call it *Devoo*, Wild Horse creek. It will take us to the Bighorn River."

Charlie lifted his eyebrows in an expression of wonder, pursed his lips and looked to Eli, "You're right, she knows this land. That's just what you said that old trapper tol' you." Charlie grinned at Bluebird, "So, you think you're gonna like travelin' with us?"

Bluebird dropped her eyes, glanced to Eli, "The McCoy's have been very nice to Squirrel and me. Did you know her grandmother was Cherokee?"

Charlie turned to look at Bluebird, glanced to Eli, "No, din't know that, but she has the look, dark hair even though it's shot with grey, high cheekbones an' such, yeah, she looks like one of us."

"Who are your people?"

"Pawnee, but my woman is white. She stayed behind to have our baby."

It was Bluebird's turn to be surprised and she turned to look at Charlie, "You did not stay with her to have your child?"

"She's gonna be with family, I needed to make some money and she wanted the space. I might make it back 'fore the youngun' comes, but mebbe not. I would be of no help nohow." Charlie's face was somber, his eyes showed he had lapsed into a moment of reminiscence.

"Well Charlie," began Eli, "now that we've got a *good* scout, if you wanna go back to be with your wife, you're free to go."

"You ain't gettin' rid o' me that easy!" declared Charlie, picking up a twig and tossing it at Eli.

By dusk, the wagons made it to the fork of Kirby Creek and another feeder creek that came from the east. This was red dirt land, but the creek that had bent to the northwest had carved a wider valley between the rambling buttes and offered good travel for the days to come. As they began making their camp at the confluence of creeks, Eli noticed the usual handful of men, pans in hand, that went to creek's edge to try to scoop a few pans full and see if they could find any color, and as usual, they were disappointed. Although they scattered out with several going upstream on the feeder creek, and others downstream on Kirby Creek, none showed any color worth mentioning.

Eli and Charlie had been invited to take supper with the McCoys and they had enjoyed a considerable meal of elk steaks, Indian potatoes, cattail shoots, and camas bulbs. Violet was beaming as the men were enjoying the meal and explained, "Squirrel showed me where to find these vegetables, aren't they good?"

"Yes'm, sure are," replied Charlie, between bites as he glanced to Eli, who was nodding his head as he ate. A glance to Max McCoy showed he was enjoying the food as well.

Violet went on to explain, "I learned so much from her already, and she also showed me some other plants that will be ready later in the season and some to stay away from!" She looked from Max to Squirrel and to Bluebird. She started to say more, but a man was coming to their wagon, looking like he had trouble on his mind, and she touched Eli's hand and said, "I think he," nodding to Felix Carpenter, one of the drivers for the trader, Catlin, who was approaching— "wants to talk to you."

Eli looked up, smiled at Violet and pushed his empty

plate forward, looked at the others, "Excuse me, please." And with a nod to Charlie, both men rose and went to meet Felix. As they neared, Felix looked about, motioned them to go between the wagons and as they gathered on the far side between the wagons and the willows, he began to explain.

"I think you're gonna have some trouble." Before he began to explain, he looked about, showing his concern about being seen and overheard, but began, "I thought it was just the usual bunch that complain 'bout ever'thin', you know the kind. There's Fisher, Fields, Hamilton among the freighters, but I saw a couple of 'em talkin' to that Dillon fella and I think his name's Sheridan. They were gripin' 'bout so many coloreds and Injuns actin' like they was takin' over the train, course we know that ain't so, but they're tryin' to stir up trouble, 'specially after you brought them girls along."

Eli shook his head, leaned back against the wagon with his arms crossed on his chest, and asked, "Did you hear if they were talkin''bout doin' somethin', or just gripin'?"

"Din't hear nothin' partic'lar, but Fields, he seems to be the leader, said they oughta do sumpin'."

Eli looked up at Felix, "Thanks Felix." Then glanced to Charlie and back to Felix, "You better go back now, circle roun' the wagons so they won't know you were here, but keep your eyes and ears open for us, will ya?"

"Yassuh, will do," replied the colored sergeant and disappeared into the darkness.

Eli looked at Charlie, "Any ideas?"

"Me think Injun should scalp 'em!" he declared, grinning, making Eli laugh. But he continued. "There's always gonna be troublemakers, but if they can't get a bunch of followers, it'll come to nothin', you know that. All we can do is wait an' see."

"Well, I think I'm going to talk to Thorne and Ryan about it, just so they'll know and might hear something before anything bad happens. That's all we need is to fight among ourselves. Right now, I think I'd as soon have some renegades attack as to deal with this kinda nonsense. At least with renegades, you know who to shoot!"

"Ummhmmm, White man shoot redskin that has feathers on his head. Just don' shoot this redskin!" grunted a grinning Charlie, mimicking the look and sounds of a disgruntled native. He laughed and added, "I'm goin' back for dessert. Mrs. McCoy said she had some pie made with some canned peaches!"

"I say we go talk to Catlin. His bunch has been trouble since the start and now they're tryin' to make more. If he can't stop it, we should leave 'em behind," declared an obstinate Nolan Thorne, shaking his head and clenching his fists. He looked to the other captain, Mark Ryan. "What do you say, Mark?"

Ryan looked at Eli. "So, you say it's couple of his drivers that were doin' this talkin'?"

"That's right."

"So, it didn't start from our people?"

"Nope, but two of the men were listenin' and agreeing. Dillon and Sheridan."

Ryan looked from Eli to Thorne. "Do we talk to them too?"

"Maybe, but we need to get Catlin to stop it. All the coloreds are with him, and the only natives are Charlie and the girls."

Eli looked at Ryan, and although he had agreed with Thorne to allow the girls to join the train, Eli was not too sure about his feelings toward any of the natives. He asked, "How do you feel about having the girls with the wagons?"

"Oh, I dunno. I didn't think having a couple girls along would be any trouble, but they are Indians and, well..." He shrugged.

"Is there something in your mind that bothers you about all Indians or just these?"

"I had some friends and family killed by some Comanche several years back. They were on a wagon train, and we didn't hear about it until a couple years later, and what we heard, well..."

Eli shook his head, "And I had friends and family killed by Whites, most were wearing uniforms of grey, so does that mean I should hate all Whites that wear grey?" growled Eli, glaring at Ryan. "Don't you think the natives have just as much reason to hate Whites? What about the Sand Creek massacre, or the Washita massacre, and others. I could stand here all day and list the different massacres where White men wiped out entire villages of men, women, and children, all because they were natives, and God forgive me, I was there at one of 'em and it made me sick to see what *civilized White men* could do to defenseless people." He looked at Ryan, shook his head, glanced at Thorne and turned away, calling over his shoulder. "I'll talk to Catlin," he growled as he stomped off.

CHAPTER 21

ABSÁALOOKE

The bounding hills on the right made Eli think of a giant caterpillar, painted with stripes of deep red ochre and buff-colored sand. He pictured the giant hand of the Creator dipping his fingers in the paints of the desert and running his fingers along the sides and tops of the hills. The colors or stripes accented the stubby fingers protruding from the long ridge and the trail followed the fingertips between the ridges and the meandering creek in the flat of the long valley. With the morning sun at their backs and the shadows of early morning stretching before them, Eli and Bluebird rode in silence, enjoying the changing colors made vibrant by the rising sun that had painted the sky's horizon edge with brilliant orange that faded to the bluish grey of early morning. It promised to be a clear day, the morning breeze was blowing softly on the land and giving the bunch grass and low growing juniper bushes a soft cadence to dance.

Bluebird looked at Eli, gave a wide sweeping motion with her arm and said, "All this is part of the Bighorn

Basin and is Crow land. From the Big Horn mountains," as she pointed to the east and northeast, "to the Owl Creek mountains," she twisted in her saddle to point to the low hills behind them to the south, "and the Absaroka Mountains," pointing to the west, "is the hunting lands of the *Absáalooke,* or Crow people."

"Are the Shoshone and Crow at peace?" asked Eli.

"Two summers past, the Crow came into the land of the Shoshone, wanting to fight and take our land from us, and they fought, and some died, but our chief, Washakie, and the chief of the Crow, Big Robber, agreed to go to the top of the butte and fight by themselves. Whoever won, the other and his people would leave. Chief Washakie came down from the butte with the heart of the Crow chief on his lance and the Crow left the land of the Wind River to be the land of the Shoshone." She paused, looked at Eli. "Now this"— waving her hand in a wide arc—"is the land of the Crow."

She dropped her eyes to her hands, remembering the times of her youth with her people and sighed, looked up and suddenly reined up her appaloosa and reached her hand to the side toward Eli. "Stop!" She nodded down the long valley and they could see a band of riders coming from a draw on the north edge that broke through the rolling hills. Eli slowly nudged his mount closer to the few alder and cottonwood that sided the creek, twisted in his saddle to retrieve his binoculars from the saddlebags and turned back to use the field glasses to get a better look at the band of riders.

"Looks to be a big hunting party, Crow probably, maybe a whole village." He handed the binoculars to Bluebird who accepted and lifted them to her eyes, jerked back when she saw the images, and slowly looked again.

"Yes, they are Crow, and it is a village. They may be going to the waters, then to hunt the buffalo."

"Waters?" asked Eli.

Bluebird grinned, nodding, pointed to the west and a little south, "On the Bighorn River, there, a place with hot waters that come from the ground, with noise and steam, and smells. Many like to bathe in them, it *does* feel good." She smiled.

"Should we stop the wagons?"

"Let us go talk to them. To talk is better than fighting."

Eli lifted his brow, nodded, grinned and waved his hand for her to lead the way. She nudged the appaloosa back to the trail and they started toward the long cavalcade of Crow people, having already been spotted by their scouts who had taken word to the leaders and were now starting to intercept the intruders to their land.

Eli noticed the band of warriors that came toward them, numbered about eight or ten, all carrying rifles, lances or bows with arrows nocked, one man who appeared to be about twenty, but rode in the front and carried only a coup stick that had many feathers and scalplocks, appeared to be the leader. As he neared, he lifted the coup stick to stop his men and to stop Eli and Bluebird. He was an impressive figure, a tall pompadour of twisted and braided hair stacked high on his head, the top portion colored white with a clay or other pigment, several feathers adorned his hair, and his leather shirt and leggings were adorned with intricate beadwork. His shirt hung open and his broad chest was adorned by a beaded breastplate of bone hairpipe. He looked from one to the other and growled in the tongue of the *Absáalooke* that was understood by Bluebird, "Why are you, a Shoshone, and this"—he snarled as he looked at Eli— "White man, in the land of the *Absáalooke?*"

"Who asks?" responded Bluebird

"I am *Alaxchíia Ahú*, Plenty Coups, war leader of the *Eelalapito Absáalooke*, Kicked in the Bellies band of the Crow people. This is the land of my people."

"We," began Bluebird, putting her hand to her chest, "are *Chosro*, Bluebird, and Elijah McCain," nodding toward Eli. "We are scouting for a wagon train of families going to the place of Three Forks, beyond the land of the *Absáalooke.*"

Eli noticed the cavalcade of the villagers had stopped and was waiting for the return or their warriors. He looked at the young leader, glanced to the others, and spoke softly to Bluebird, "Translate for me. I will use sign."

She glanced to Eli, responded softly, "He understands English, I know of him. His name is Plenty Coups and is a respected leader of his people."

Eli nodded, and began, using sign and pausing to let Bluebird translate for all that were there. "I am the leader of the wagon train. There are many families and some men that are going to set up a trading post in the land near the Three Forks. You will be welcome to come and trade there. We will only pass through your land and only take such game as necessary for food."

Plenty Coups scowled, looking from Eli to Bluebird, then nudged his mount forward to ride between them, looking at their gear and the packs on the grey. As he passed Eli, he tapped him lightly on the shoulder with his coup stick, but Eli did not respond and Plenty Coups rode back to the front of his band, turned to face Eli, "You have more than one rifle. What if I take them all before you go?"

"You could try, but you will die," answered Eli, a stoic expression on his face as he glared back at the young warrior. "I have fought in many battles, in the War between the States, and in fights with Lakota, Cheyenne, Arapaho, Comanche, and Blackfoot. And I have never been beaten. It is because I have strong medicine and am not afraid of my enemies, but I would rather be a friend to the Crow as I am a friend to the Shoshone, the Salish, the Blackfoot, the Pawnee, the Comanche and others."

As Eli spoke, using his hands for sign and speaking confidently and slowly, Bluebird rapidly translated his words to the other warriors, but watched the movements and reaction of all the warriors as she spoke the words of the White man beside her. She was thrilled with his words and his confidence and that he responded from a position of strength and command, as she translated, she sat taller, her shoulders back and her head high, letting a slow grin paint her face. When he finished, she looked at Plenty Coups, saw his stern expression, but knew he would not act foolishly for he had already established himself as a confident and wise leader that would someday be a chief of the *Absáalooke* people.

With a nod, Plenty Coups held up his hand, palm open and facing Eli, and said, "It is good." He reined his mount to the side and led his men back to the people at a walk.

Eli and Bluebird sat watching for a moment, then Bluebird looked at Eli. "Have you been in that many battles?"

Eli nodded, keeping his eyes on the warriors. "Ummhmm."

Bluebird smiled, cocked her head to the side. "You are a good man, a brave man, and I am proud to say I know you and am your friend."

He looked at her, let a smile break his face, and he said, "Perhaps more," and chuckled.

His words filled Bluebird with wonder and hope, and she breathed deeply, smiling at the one she hoped would one day be her man.

He nudged Rusty back to the edge of the trees, stepped down and looked at Bluebird as she did the same. He loosened the girths of the claybank and the grey, slipped their bridles off and used the lead ropes of the bosals to tether the animals, picked a spot in the shade and watched as Bluebird began gathering some wood to make a fire for some coffee. They would wait for the wagons and use this place for nooning, giving the Crow people time to pass.

CHAPTER 22

BIGHORN

They rode into the sunset as the trail took them north of the mouth of the Wind River canyon and the confluence of the Wind River and the Bighorn. Now it was just the deeper, broader, meandering Bighorn River that flowed north and would be their companion for the next few days of travel. But for now, it was to be the refreshing stop promised a few days back, and the women were looking forward to time to wash clothes, have their men get a bath and to bathe themselves.

The mouth of the valley that held Kirby Creek opened wide to show the stretch of green that rode the shoulders of the Bighorn River. The gold of the setting sun brushed the tops of the cottonwoods and the crests of the hills to the north and east of the river. The chuckle of the river, the rattle of leaves in the breeze and the occasional cry of red-wing blackbirds and hawks as they searched for their supper, filled the air with a cacophony of sound that blended and harmonized as the finest wilderness symphony. The ratatat of a woodpecker, the rapid rattle of the cuckoo, and the sweet tweets of the warbler added to the music. Eli and Bluebird sat their mounts, leaning on the pommels of their saddles and savoring the view and the moment.

The crack of a bullwhip brought them out of their reverie and Eli led the way to what would be the crossing, but they would not ford the water until after their time of rest. He signaled the lead wagon to make the circle at the edge of the trees, and the tired animals lifted their heads at the sight of greenery and the smell of fresh water. Eli motioned to Bluebird to follow him upstream while the wagons made their camp, knowing Charlie, who had been on the flank and backtrail most of the day would find them and make the report. In the meantime, Eli was looking forward to some hot coffee.

———

Čhetáŋ KiŋYáŋ, Flying Hawk, was the leader of the band of Sioux that had followed the wagon train with the trader Catlin who had promised rifles for the people. Although his band had numbered about forty warriors, they had visited the village of the Brule and Oglala under Spotted Tail and Young Man Afraid of his Horses and other warriors who had joined them. Most had been a part of Red Cloud's war, but many had disagreed with Red Cloud and the treaty signed at Fort Laramie. Since the people did not believe that one man could speak for another, they believed the treaty did not include them.

After conferring with Spotted Tail and the others, Flying Hawk's older brothers, Kicking Bear and Black Fox II, all sons of Chief Black Fox or Great Kicking Bear, and their cousins, Eagle Thunder and Walking Eagle, joined the band that would pursue the trader's wagons and take the promised rifles and more. Flying Hawk believed their band would now number five or six double hands, fifty to sixty, of warriors, a good number.

Kicking Bear was also a Holy Man and yielded the leadership of the band to Flying Hawk, but the cousins together made up the leadership of the band and now as they were ready to break camp where they had spent the night at the confluence of Kirby Creek and Lake Creek, the same site where the wagons had camped earlier, they joined together to confer about their plan.

"We are almost two days behind, if we are to take them, we must hurry," began Flying Hawk, looking around the circle.

"They have as many shooters as do we, we must be wise in our attack," suggested Kicking Bear. "I believe our medicine is good, the signs are with us, but we must be wise."

Eagle Thunder added, "On our early scout, we saw many of the men go to the stream with their pans to look for the gold, they are most often alone. It would be good to have some of our warriors to take them, quietly, before we attack the wagons."

"And we could take their horses after dark, that would force them to stay with their wagons," stated Walking Eagle.

The others nodded, grunted in agreement until Flying Hawk said, "If we take those at the stream before we take the horses, they will be on their guard, and if we take the horses first, they will also be on their guard."

"It would be best to wait until we kill them all to take the horses," stated Black Fox.

Flying Hawk said, "Let us go, after dark we will move closer, and they will not expect an attack. When they take their morning meal, they are not watching for an attack. We can get close, hit from all sides, and make a short fight of it all."

"Then let us ride, we must move without waiting," stated Kicking Bear. The others looked around, nodded, and went to their horses. As they were readying to leave, a small band of Oglala warriors numbering about ten or twelve, came into their camp, and the leader, Short Bull, said, "We have come to join you!"

———

IT WAS A VERY haggard and tired Charlie that rode into the camp of Eli and Bluebird. He slid to the ground, dropped on his rear and looked at Eli, "I think we got trouble comin'!" Bluebird handed him a cup of hot steaming coffee, took the lead of his horse and led the animal to water. While she stripped the animal of its gear, the buckskin savored the water and the grass, and enjoyed the rubdown that Bluebird was giving him with a handful of dry grass. She picketed the horse and moved back to the fire, seating herself near Eli and listening to Charlie.

"I got close enough to see they were Sioux, probably Oglala. I think they were the same ones that followed us and were after the rifles from Catlin. But they have more'n they had before, I'm guessin' they got mebbe fifty-sixty warriors, maybe more. And if they want, they can catch up just any time now," explained Charlie, sipping on the steaming coffee and looking at Eli over the rim of the cup.

"What makes you think they're after us?" asked Eli.

"I did not see any scouts, 'cep'n two out front. No hunters, no wanderin' about lookin' for tracks. Stayed right on our trail."

"And with us takin' a day of rest and washin' up an' such, they could be on us just anytime," surmised Eli.

"Ummhmm," agreed Charlie, sipping at his coffee. "What'chu think we oughta be doin'?"

"Don't wanna alarm the folks, but you'n me, maybe a couple others'll stand watch through the night, then we'll move across the river in the mornin', maybe go a little further upstream and find a better site that we can defend, then let 'em have their day of rest or..." he shrugged. "I'll walk through the camp, let folks know the change in plans, listen to their gripes, and we'll be ready to move out 'fore first light. You and I will stand first watch, maybe to about midnight, then get some rest. I want you and whoever you choose, maybe one of those youngun's, to watch our backtrail. I don't think we'll hafta move more'n half a day upstream, but we'll just have to wait and see. Me'n Bluebird will be ridin' point."

Charlie stood, tossed out the dregs of his coffee, stretched, "Then I reckon I need to go into camp, pick my lookouts, maybe get somethin' to eat, and..." he shrugged, grinning. "Since I don't have me a woman, reckon I'll just hafta make do with muh supper."

Eli laughed, "We both been invited to dinner with the Proctor's, that'll give you a chance to talk to Ted, if he's one you want."

Charlie grinned, "He is, and his momma is a mighty fine cook!" he declared.

Eli chuckled and looked at Bluebird, "And you're goin' to the McCoy wagon, right?"

She smiled coyly, "Since *I* don't have an invitation to any other camp, I guess I am."

Eli grinned, pulled her close to his side, and the three started for the wagons. As they neared the wagons, Bluebird separated from the men, and Eli looked to Charlie.

"I think I'll talk to Catlin, see if he's got'ny spare rifles, maybe pass 'em out, or have 'em ready, just in case. And since the Sioux are on our tail, he might try to make contact with 'em like he did before. He deserves watching."

"You go right ahead, while you're talkin' to him, I think I'll talk to Felix, kinda give him and his men a head's up so they can be ready. Those boys are good fightin' men."

"They are that, but tell 'em to keep it to themselves."

"Oh, they'll do that alright. But if Catlin has any rifles to spare, Felix will probably know all about 'em."

"That gives me an idea, maybe I'll just ask him about gettin' a rifle for Bluebird, that might tip his hand."

Charlie chuckled, "Now you're buyin' things for her, what next? A wedding ring?"

CHAPTER 23

OGLALA

The night was overcast, and the clouds hid most of the stars and blanketed the moon. It did not bode well for the coming day, and they would have to move out before first light. While crossing most streams was nothing to be concerned about, the Bighorn River was more than what they had crossed before, but the crossing was well marked, broad, and with a firm gravel bottom, and Eli was optimistic about the crossing, *as long as it doesn't break out in a cloudburst and flood things!* He shook his head at the thought.

Eli had spoken to the two captains of the train, Nolan Thorne and Mark Ryan, to let them know about the Sioux and their need to find a better, more defensible camp. The Proctor wagon led off and started into the water, what promised to be an easy crossing began without incident as the Proctor wagon crossed the shallows before the island, made it across the island and dropped into deeper water that crowded the box of the wagon, pushed at the wheels and covered the smaller front wheels. The horses, a four-up, leaned into the harness and collars, digging deep as Jerry Proctor cracked the whip over their heads. As they pushed across, the horses soon found more solid footing, climbed the slight slope of the exit ramp and were soon free of the water. Jerry pushed them further up the road, pulled to the side, locked the brake, stepped down and went to each of the horses, checking the harness and stroking their necks and talking easily to them. He was proud of his team and told them so as he ran his fingers through their manes. This had been the first true test of both team and wagon, and he was relieved.

The other wagons followed, proved themselves capable, and the train continued to make the crossing. But after the heavier trade wagons crossed the island, the soil was getting churned by the digging of hooves of the many teams and the remaining wagons had a greater challenge. Eli noticed as the last of the trader's wagons and their four-up teams of big mules came from the water, it seemed the river level was rising. He looked to the south to see black storm clouds hanging over the hills and the veil of a rainstorm showed above the distant low-rising peaks. He looked back at the water, saw it showing a hint of mud, and knew the floodwaters were coming. The last three wagons were those of McCoy, Thorne, and Ryan.

He dug heels to a reluctant Rusty and went back into the water to get the other wagons moving. They had been sitting idle, waiting for the trader's wagons to get across, and now that the last of those had crossed, they needed to get moving. When he pushed Rusty up the far bank, he saw the ladies sitting on the driver's seats, but the men were nowhere to be seen. He saw Violet McCoy with Squirrel on the driver's seat of the first wagon,

Violet holding the lead lines, and Eli asked, "Where's Max and the others?"

"Oh, since they had to sit an' wait, Nolan and Mark wanted to try their luck and pannin' and Max went along to watch." She shook her head and mumbled something Eli could not quite hear but he knew she was not happy with her man.

"Where'd they go?" asked Eli.

Violet pointed upstream to the south of the crossing. "Thataway some'eres."

Eli nodded and dug heels to Rusty and took off through the cottonwoods, searching the banks for the three men. He spotted Max standing behind one of the men and hollered, "Max! Get to your wagon—you've got to get across 'fore the stormwaters come!"

The big man turned, frowning, looked where Eli was pointing, turned back wide-eyed, nodding, "Youbetcha!" and he took off at a trot to get to his wagon.

Down on his knees at water's edge, Mark Ryan was washing a pan of mud and rocks and Eli reined Rusty close, "You willin' to trade your wagon and family for a few flakes of gold?" he growled, leaning on his pommel to scowl at Mark.

The man turned, looked at Eli, "Huh? What'chu mean?"

"If you don't get your wagon across 'fore the stormwater hits, you ain't gonna make it and that band of Sioux will hang your scalp and those of your family from their war lances and right soon!"

Mark stood, tossed the pan full of silt and more into the river, and started back to his wagon at a run, but Eli hollered, "Where's Nolan?"

Mark stopped, turned and pointed upstream, "Thataway!"

In just a few minutes, Eli had fetched Nolan Thorne, shook his head disgustedly and mumbled, "Gold fever!"

———

IT HAD TAKEN a good two plus hours for the wagons to make the crossing, the most difficult being the last wagon of Nolan Thorne's that had bogged down in the churned soil of the island and had to have help from the spare team of the trader, but once across, everyone was relieved and looking forward to their final stop for the day, which Eli had promised would give them ample daylight for their many chores, but the storm was coming north and following the river. The thunder was rolling across the dark sky, and lances of blue were stabbing at the hills, threatened the train, but it was later in the morning when the clouds opened and began their downpour. Eli was concerned about Charlie and his two fellow scouts, Ted Proctor and Zeke Tabor.

Eli kept the wagons on the move, but he and Bluebird still scouted ahead, looking for the right site that would give them the best defensive position. After about six or seven miles, the river made a swooping bend to the northeast around the nose of a long high ridge. With the bend of the river, the hills behind it and the trees along the bank, this was the spot that would be perfect. He pointed out the bend to Bluebird, "The animals will be kept in with the trees and the river, we'll make the wagons do a horseshoe bend out thisaway, and you and I will get on that ridge yonder, and, yeah, that'll do just fine."

She smiled, holding her new Henry .44 that Eli bought from the trader, across the pommel of her saddle and looked wide-eyed at Eli, nodding in agreement.

They wheeled the horses around and moved back away from the trees, went to the road and waited for the wagons. As they neared, he went alongside the first wagon and instructed him to go to the edge of the trees, pull his wagon in close before unharnessing the horses, and the rest would make a horseshoe bend around the grassy flat. He gave each wagon the instructions, watched as they began to form up and sat, leaning on the pommel, as he glanced from the wagons to Bluebird and back.

The men were doing as instructed, moving the wagons as close to one another as possible, usually having to use manpower to pull the wagons as close as instructed, but once done, the semi-circle made a well-fortified defensive line. Eli called everyone together and began. "I know the word has probably already circulated among you all that the band of Sioux that had followed us before is still behind us, and looking a little more dangerous. Charlie said they have more warriors than before, and they've been staying on our tail. He thought they might go after the Shoshone, but they stayed on our trail, which tells me they have plans to attack." He paused, looking around at the expressions of the people, some showed fear, others anger, all showed concern. Eli continued, "Now, I believe we have a good defensive position here. The animals will be safe between the wagons and the river, the wagons are close and will be easily defended, and in the meantime, ladies, feel free to go to the river to do whatever you need to do, I'll make sure there will be someone always on guard." He paused again. "Now, we don't know when or even if they'll attack, but we must always be watchful. If they do, it will be because they want our horses, our weapons, and... well, whatever else might be enticing to them." He looked at the women and knew they understood what he meant.

"Now, if any of you ladies know how to shoot, make sure you have a weapon. If you don't have one, maybe the trader will loan you one, he has some he planned on putting in his mercantile store, but tryin' 'em out is always good. Just don't be out of reach of your weapon, and as for you men," He shook his head, "Even if the bottom of that river was solid gold, it won't be worth sacrificing your family and your own life for something you won't live long enough to enjoy!" He looked around at a few of the men who dropped their eyes, looked to the ground, shuffling their feet and mumbling, "Do I make myself clear?"

Most of the men nodded their heads, some even pulled their wives closer, and Eli knew those that cared, understood, but he also knew there would be some that just could not or would not resist the clarion call of gold fever.

Eli looked up, saw the dust of three riders and knew that Charlie and company were coming into the camp, and he dismissed the others, "Now, keep watch, but do your business 'fore anything else happens." He looked to the sky, saw the storm clouds moving to the west and knew they would be spared at least this much of the aggravation for the day.

Charlie and the two youngsters reined up at the edge of the wagons on the south side, stepped down just as Bluebird and Eli came from between a couple wagons. Eli waved the three to the edge of the trees and gathered them around in a small clearing. They seated themselves on a couple downed cottonwood logs and Eli asked, "So?"

"They're comin' alright. Looks to be maybe seventy-five or so."

"Ooooee, they've been recruitin' some others. Probably on the promise of easy takin's and plenty of weapons."

Charlie nodded, "And these ain't all young bucks out to prove themselves, there's some older chiefs or war leaders among 'em."

"How soon you think they'll get here?"

"If they push it, like they're might to, they'll be here 'bout dusk, a good time for an attack."

"Ummhmmm," nodded Eli, looking down, focusing his thoughts. He looked up to Charlie, "I'm gonna climb that point yonder behind them and across the river to the crown of the ridge that stood about a hundred feet or more above the flats and offered a good view of what lay below. "Me'n Bluebird will guard this end of things 'case they try to come around that point and cross the river to attack from that side. I want you three spaced along the riverbank all along here," he pointed to the bank that backed up the wagons and horse herd. "They'll prob'ly try to come around that end, and hit from the river. If an' when you start shootin', I'll have a few of the men ready to come reinforce you. But they'll be stationed along the arc of the wagons." He paused, looked at the three. "Now, go get somethin' to eat 'fore things start."

Chapter 24

Company

Eli stood before the people, standing on a wooden crate, and began, "We need to have at least two shooters 'tween each of the wagons. Husband/wife, youngsters, other men, whoever, but you need to try to alternate your shootin', that way you won't be defenseless when one has to reload or whatever. The Sioux are known to be fierce fighters and they'll come at us horseback, crawlin' through the grass an' sage, any way they can, so keep your eye sharp and always be ready." He looked around the group, and continued, "Charlie and the boys say the Sioux could be here as early as dusk, so we need to be ready by that time. Try to fortify your spaces, put boxes and such under the wagons so they can't crawl through there, and give yourselves some protection to stand behind. Now, they might not attack right away, but we can't get careless."

Someone spoke from the crowd, "If we make it till dark, will we be alright?"

Another one said, "Yeah, an' they won't crawl through all that cactus out there, will they?"

Eli chuckled. "They're just as prone to attack in the night as in the day. Whenever they think they have the advantage, they'll attack, and some of 'em like fightin' at night better'n day. And as for that cactus, that's the very reason they will crawl through it, because you think they won't and won't expect 'em. Now, let's get to work and make ready!" He motioned to the two captains and gathered with them near the trees. He pointed to the bluff on the far side of the river. "I'm gonna be up there with Bluebird, we'll be guarding this end of the flank, try to keep 'em from comin' 'round behind and crossin' the river to get to the horses. Charlie and the boys will be along these trees, closer to the water to cover the back and that flank, yonder," he said, pointing downstream. "I need you to pick a couple two, three men, that if they hear shooting coming from the river, for them to break away and reinforce Charlie and the boys. If the shooting is from the bluff, don't worry about it." He looked from one to the other, "Nolan, I need you to walk along behind the shooters, back 'em up if need be, but keep 'em focused and don't let any of 'em fire until you give the word. Sure enough, somebody will get nervous, think he sees somethin' and shoots, and they'll waste a lot of ammunition on jackrabbits and coyotes!"

The two men looked at one another, back to Eli and both nodded and agreed. Mark Ryan said, "I'll get a couple men to back up the boys while you walk the line and let the folks know what we need to do, you know, 'bout shootin' together an' such."

Nolan nodded, looked to Eli and extended his hand, "I just wanna thank you for what you're doin' 'fore things get outta hand. We couldn'ta made it this far without'chu."

Eli grinned, shook his hand. "You've got more salt in

you than you realize. There's a lot of good folks here and together, they'll make quite an army. Just remember, those coloreds with Catlin, they're all experienced soldiers, fought with the 10th Cavalry, you can depend on them. You might want to put them at any weak spot you find."

Nolan grinned, nodded, "Will do." He looked at Mark and said, "Let's go," and started to make his survey of the people and their positions and fortifications.

Eli walked over to the trader's wagons and motioned Felix to join him. They walked toward the trees together and Eli asked, "Would you help out Nolan Ryan? He's one of the captains and he'll be ramroddin' the defense, but I don't think he's been in any scrapes like this."

"What'chu wan' me tado?" asked Felix, thinking back to his days with the 10th at Fort Hays and the many skirmishes he and his men had with different bands of Sioux, Kiowa, and Comanche.

"I told him to keep the shooting spaced out, you know, so there's always a ready shooter at each gap, and to not let 'em start shootin' too soon. I told him about you and the others that were with the 10th, and I think he'd like to have some experience walkin' with him."

"I can do that. I'll hafta let Mr. Catlin know, but I reckon that'd be alright."

"Good. I'm gonna be up on that butte yonder, guardin' the flank. The Sioux are always wanting to get the horses, and with them back here near the river, I figger they'll try to come from behind, but we'll be ready up there to kinda discourage 'em," he chuckled, put his hand on Felix' shoulder and said, "Thanks, you're a good man, Felix." The colored former sergeant grinned, gave a casual salute, turned and said, "Thanks Colonel!"

―――――

ELI AND BLUEBIRD picketed their horses in the slight basin behind the shoulder of the butte, well out of sight of anyone that was not atop the butte. Eli carried his Spencer and the Winchester Yellow Boy, a possibles pouch with ammunition, and his binoculars in the case hung from one shoulder. Bluebird carried her new Henry, a pouch of ammunition, and her bow and arrows were in the quiver at her back. They worked their way over the slight shoulder toward the west facing rimrock of the butte. As they paused for a better survey, Eli saw the rimrock was in layers and what appeared to offer the best promontory and cover was the bench just below the larger layer of rimrock and less than a hundred feet from the crest.

As they began to position themselves, Eli looked below at the base of the butte, calculating the distance to be less than two hundred yards to anyone in the scattered piñon and beyond that to the far side of the river at the tree line to be about three hundred yards. A bit too far for the Winchester, but not for the Spencer. They began stacking some loose shale and rocks for better cover and to use as a support, but Eli paused, looked upriver and slipped the binoculars from the case and began to search the back trail.

"Ummhmm, here they come. Charlie was right, it'll be about dusk 'fore they get in any position."

Eli cupped his hands, looked toward the trees where he suspected Charlie had positioned himself, and gave the loud whistle like *peent* call of the nighthawk, followed by the deep-throated *boom* the bird was known to use. He saw Charlie step from the trees, looking his way with his hand shading his eyes, and Eli motioned upstream, nodding, giving both hands, all fingers extended, twice, to indicate about twenty minutes away. Charlie nodded, turned back into the trees and disappeared.

Eli had cupped his hat over the binoculars to ensure no reflected light from the setting sun would give him away, and hunkered down for a longer and more thorough look. He spoke to Bluebird, "Charlie was right, there's a big bunch of 'em. I reckon they'll send scouts, if they haven't already, and make their plan. Then we'll see if they're gonna attack soon, or wait, or how they'll come at us." He lowered his binoculars and turned to look at Bluebird who sat with the Henry lying over her crossed legs and looking at Eli.

She smiled, "I am glad to be with you," she scooted a little closer to him, reached out to touch his knee and nodded to the trees below. "Do you want me to shoot when they are there?"

"No, I want you to keep watch all about," he handed her the binoculars. "While I'm focused on anybody comin' this way"—pointing below them—"I don't want others sneakin' around behind us, maybe tryin' to get up here so they can shoot down into the wagons or comin' after us. You need to keep 'em off my back."

"I will," she stated, a stoic expression painting her face as she accepted the binoculars.

The sun was lowering over the rolling hills and flat-top mesas in the west, sending shafts of gold across the remaining blues of the afternoon sky, and painting the bellies of the few clouds that hung lazily over the western lands. Under other circumstances, Eli would have considered the time and the country beautiful, but the lengthening shadows and coming of dusk carried a foreboding blanket that covered the land. Eli had lain out his rifles, ammunition within easy reach, and turned to face Bluebird who was scanning the south as she watched the war party of Sioux. She quietly spoke into the evening breeze, "That is Kicking Bear, he is a Holy Man, and the other is Flying Hawk, his brother, a known war leader. They are splitting—as you thought, some are going to the river to come this way, most are staying near the road."

She handed the binoculars to Eli, and he lifted them to spot the different groups. The smaller group, numbering about fifteen or twenty, moved close to the trees beside the river. He scanned the river bed, saw that where the river pushed against the hills, it would be impossible for them to side the river on the near side without crossing over and climbing the hills, but closer to his position, they could and probably would, cross and follow the near bank to come at the flank of the wagons just below his position.

He looked back to the larger band who were still out of sight of the wagons, but it appeared they would follow the road until it made the bend around the point of the butte and the bend in the river, then make their attack. They could easily stretch out along the road and come at the arc of the wagons with a broad front, hitting the entire train with an all-out attack. *That's what I'd do, anyway,* thought Eli. He handed the binoculars back to Bluebird and said, "They're comin'!" He cupped his hands to make another nighthawk call to warn Charlie and the others, then hunkered down behind the rocks and lifted his Spencer. He remembered those in the war called Berdan's Sharpshooters and thought, *I'd like to have one of their telescopic sights 'bout now, but wishful thinking never won any battles.*

He looked below to see the band of about twenty warriors coming to river's edge and begin to split up.

They were about a mile away, but he watched as half the warriors crossed the river, quickly crossed the flats below the buttes, and take to a draw that split the buttes and would probably give them a way over the hills behind them and to the river below the wagon camp. The rest started through the trees, following the north bank of the river and coming his way. He bellied down, lined out his Spencer and sighted in on the trees at the narrowing of the trail at the base of the butte. He waited for them to draw near, and Bluebird said, "The others are coming around the point of the bend. They will be in sight of the wagons soon."

Eli knew if he fired, it would probably begin the battle, and he wanted to wait as long as possible for everything to be in place and not have random shooting going on that would add to any confusion that always seemed to be a part of a battle. He looked to the horizon, saw the shadows of the hills and the large band of Sioux rounding the point. *If they start the attack, I'll open the ball down here.* Keeping his eye on the nearest group, he glanced to the larger bunch and Bluebird spoke, "I hear the others behind us, but they are not near."

Eli nodded, looked below and saw the group picking their way through the scattered juniper and piñon, surreptitiously making their way to the river. "If we start shooting before they get to the river, they might come over the hill at us, so be ready!"

CHAPTER 25

BATTLE

I t was a tactic used to instill fear in their enemies and it was effective now. The main force of the Oglala stretched out in a long line across the expanse of the flat before the wagons, and slowly began to walk their mounts toward the wagons. They believed they were out of range of the White man's rifles, and they were accustomed to fighting forces that had the single shot Springfield muzzleloaders that used the .58 caliber minnie ball and were the most common weapon of the war and was also the standard issue of the western forts. But unknown to the Sioux, most of the shooters with the wagons were outfitted with Spencer repeaters or Henry repeaters, which was done at the insistence of Eli before they left Fort Laramie.

When Eli saw the long line begin its approach, he saw those below readying to cross the river. He had mentally marked a landmark of brush and rocks in the flats between the wagons and the warriors, saw them near it and brought his Spencer to full cock, picked his target, a warrior that appeared to be in the lead of the band below, dropped the hammer and the Spencer bucked, blasted, spat smoke, fire and lead and the battle began. Eli saw the targeted warrior slide from his mount and fall into the water at river's edge, all while Eli was picking another target and bringing the Spencer to full cock.

His shot started the battle. He saw the line of warriors lift lances, hawks, war shields and weapons and kick their mounts to a gallop, but at the same time, the long line of rifles at the wagons barked in unison and several of the attackers were knocked from the horses, to be trampled under the hooves of those behind them. The cloud of smoke lay before the wagons, but the second shooters had picked their targets and staggered firing began to take its toll. The screams of war cries, the thunder of hooves, the roar of rifles blasting filled the air with a cacophony of noise that scattered every bird that sat in the trees, the deer that had picked their beds and the horses that were milling around in their pasture.

Eli's second shot took its toll and his third took another warrior in his shoulder, making him drop his muzzleloader and slide to the ground. The continuous barrage from the wagons stayed the attack and the natives began to slow in their charge, several turning back to avoid the hail of lead that came like waves on the lakes, no let-up and constant. Each man had seen many of his fellow warriors fall, most felt the whispering of bullets passing them, and several horses had been killed, forcing the downed warriors to either continue the fight on foot, or accept the hand of a passing warrior that would lift him from the ground, allowing him to swing aboard behind the rider.

Bluebird called out, "Behind us!" and lifted her Henry and fired, jacked another round and fired again. Eli grabbed his Winchester as he turned and lifted but was driven back by the lunge of a warrior, warhawk lifted high and screaming his war cry. Eli lifted his Winchester to block the attack, feeling the hawk strike the barrel, but Eli brought the butt of the rifle up to strike the jaw of the attacker, knocking him to the ground. But the warrior was quick to regain his feet, dropped into a crouch, hawk lifted and glaring at Eli who brought the muzzle of the Winchester toward the warrior, pulled the trigger, and the rifle did not fire and the warrior screamed and charged, driving Eli to his back, still holding the rifle between them.

Bluebird had dropped three attackers, wounded another, and was kept busy keeping the others from getting close. She jacked another round, fired, again and again, saw blood blossom on three chests, another take a bullet in the neck and choke on his own blood, and two others turn away to find cover. The scream of the warrior behind her brought her around to see the warrior astraddle of Eli, one hand of the warrior holding the rifle down which pinned Eli's hands, and the other hand with the hawk lifted high. The warrior screamed again, but the bullet from Bluebird's Henry made him arch his back, as the bullet exited through his chest and shattered the bone hairpipe breastplate and showered Eli with blood. The warrior slumped forward, pinning Eli but Eli quickly twisted and squirmed out from under him.

Eli looked at Bluebird who stood staring at the dead warrior, looked to Eli and both looked to the other dead warriors, saw the few left alive scampering down the hill and both slumped to the ground, staring at one another, until Bluebird began to smile and said, "We made it!"

Eli chuckled, came to his knees and looked about, saw the scattered remains of warriors and horses both below the butte and beyond the wagons, and said, "I think we've all made it." He knew that many were killed, but not all those thought to be dead were left behind. Many had been wounded and carried away or crawled away, even those near the bunker of Eli and Bluebird had been dragged away, all except the one that had fought with Eli.

As the tide of battle turned and the attacking Sioux fell back, those below the butte that had been dropped by lead from Eli's Spencer, had also turned back and he saw most of the attackers were fleeing, although they had retrieved those fallen warriors, some of whom were probably still alive though grievously wounded. He knew, if given the opportunity, the warriors would return after dark and retrieve the bodies of their dead warriors and he would encourage the people of the wagons to allow them to be taken.

Eli looked at Bluebird, picked up the binoculars for a quick scan of the battlefield, even though the light was fading, and satisfied, said, "Let's go down to the wagons, see what all happened down there."

As they crossed the river, they were met by a grinning Charlie, "Well, looks like we showed 'em!" he declared, glancing to see the two young men, Ted and Zeke, coming through the trees. He called out to them, "You fellas alright?"

"Yeah, we only had a couple try to cross, think we kilt one. The other'n run off," responded Zeke, grinning at Charlie and Eli.

"Yeah, we accounted for a few also," answered Charlie. He looked up at Eli and said, "Heard you two doin' a bunch a' shootin' up there."

"Yeah, we had some down here wantin' to cross the river, and others came up behind us, but Bluebird stopped 'em." He turned and grinned at Bluebird who sat with her Henry across the pommel, a somber expression painting her face.

Eli said, "Let's go check on the pilgrims," and pushed Rusty into the trees to go to the wagons, followed closely by the others. Eli stepped down, stripped their horses of their gear and let them loose to join the herd. After stacking their gear with the packs previously placed in a likely campsite at the edge of the trees, he caught up with Charlie. The boys left to check on their families and Bluebird went to the McCoy's to check on her sister.

As they came to the trader's wagons, they saw one of the men, Skunk Hoxie, was dead from an arrow through the throat, and the ramrod, Dre Jackson, had taken a lance in his leg that one of the other coloreds, Eustice Green, was tending. Eli saw Felix, asked, "Anyone else hurt?"

"You mean among the freighters? Nah, that's all. But there's some o' them other folks wit' duh wagons got a little blooded. You might wanna check on 'em."

"Doin' that now. Thanks for helpin' Thorne, most of the folks done a bang-up job!"

Felix grinned broadly, "Yassuh, most of 'em done that," he chuckled.

The Proctor wagon was at the northernmost end of the line and Ted had already made it to his family's wagon, and stood grinning, proud of his family and himself. When Charlie neared, he said, "We showed 'em, din't we? Pa said he got one, mebbe two and Ma hit one too!" He looked from Charlie and Eli to his folks who were seated on a box, Jerry busy reloading the two rifles.

Charlie grinned. "Sounds good, but don't let your guard down, they might be back."

His statement brought a sudden frown to Ted's face and stopped Jerry in his actions as he looked up at Charlie. "You really think they'll be back?" he asked incredulously.

"You can't ever tell. Usually when they lose this many," began Charlie, nodding to the flats where several bodies of both men and horses lay, "they'll think whatever we have won't be worth losin' more, but you can't ever tell. They might just be mad enough to try again."

Jerry looked at his wife Sarah, then to Ted, and said, "We'll just hafta do it!" He set the rifle aside and took his wife in his arms, she sobbed into his chest, sagged in his arms, and they both sat down, clinging tightly to one another.

Most of the others had the same response, relief at the stopped attack, but fear at the possibility of another. When they came to the wagon of Zeke, he was sitting at a makeshift table where his mother lay her head and was sobbing. Zeke looked at the two men, shook his head, "Pa was killed, took an arrow in the back," he stated simply, nodding to the covered body that lay beneath the wagon. "He thought he'd shoot better from there, but one of 'em came close, saw him and done him in. Ma said he got a couple 'fore he went under."

Jim Dillon, the father of two young boys had fought alongside his wife, the boys stayed in the wagon, but he had taken an arrow in the shoulder and his wife, Emma, was tending him. Charlie stepped close. "Let me help you with that, ma'am. I done this afore. You get that knife yonder, get it red hot if'n you will." Eli took the knife from the woman and went to a small fire she had started to make coffee, and stuck the blade into the hot coals. She sat down on a crate, and with elbows on her knees, she watched Charlie as he cut the shaft of the arrow, and looked at Eli. "That knife 'bout ready?"

Eli nodded, knelt down by the fire, put his hand on

the hilt of the knife and looked back at Charlie. Charlie spoke to Jim, "This is gonna hurt, but that knife's hot and we'll need to cauterize the wound, both front n' back. So sink yore teeth in this."

He handed him the leather scabbard for the knife. When he was ready, he nodded, and Charlie quickly pulled the shaft of the arrow out through his back, nodded to Eli who lay the hot blade against the wound at his chest, turned it over and did the same to the wound at his back. Jim gritted his teeth on the scabbard, squinted his eyes and moaned as he gripped the edge of the board he sat on. He breathed deep, dropped his head and relaxed his mouth to let the scabbard drop. He looked up at Charlie and Eli, "Thanks, men."

Charlie looked to Emma, "You need to watch that wound, make sure it don't fester. If it starts to, you need to lance it, clean it, put some whiskey on it, and bandage it good."

"We don't have any whiskey," pleaded Emma.

Eli said, "I'll send Bluebird over with some Balm of Gilead. It's a good remedy that'll help."

A few others, one woman, two men, had minor wounds, but the rest were just weary and fearful of any more attacks. It would be a restless night, but Eli assured them if the Sioux did not attack by morning, they were probably safe to leave. That little bit of hope did wonders.

CHAPTER 26

TRAIL

They stood in the dark, outside the arc of the wagons, waiting. The moon was waxing full, and their eyes were accustomed to the dim moonlight, but they kept behind the cover of bunches of sage, greasewood, and Bluebird stood beside a gnarled piñon. While Eli was nearby and had her within sight, Charlie was farther to the south, closer to the bend of the river. Scattered before them among the sage, bunch grass, and cacti, were the bodies of warriors that had fallen in the attack, at least one still living as his moans filled the darkness with haunting sounds of impending death. They knew the Sioux would come for their dead and wounded, and Bluebird believed she could convince them to leave with their dead and not return.

The watchers were unmoving, still, and quiet and the sounds of approaching horses picking their way through the bushes told of their coming. As they neared, Eli guessed there were maybe six or eight, but more horses than men. The natives separated, looking for their downed warriors, until the clear voice of Bluebird broke the stillness. She spoke in the tongue of the Lakota, "You have come for your dead, that is good. Take them and go in peace. I am *Chosro*, a shaman of the *Tukkutikka* Shoshone. Our medicine is strong, stronger than that of Kicking Bear and our warriors have rifles that fire many times, our war leaders know about Flying Hawk, but we go from this place and choose to go in peace. If you come again, we will not stop with the killing of your people, your women will weep and cut themselves and many will die. It does not have to be that way. You have lost many, go in peace and let this be the end."

The night air carried her words clearly and as she spoke, the band of warriors had frozen in place, and when her voice fell quiet, the sounds of movement told they were gathering the bodies. Bluebird had moved away in the darkness, moving closer to where Eli waited, but neither Eli nor Charlie had spoken, and their shadows blended with those of the sage and the warriors did not know of their presence. Eli watched as one of the men left his horse and picked his way stealthily through the brush and cacti, making his way to the lone tree where Bluebird had been. Eli grinned when the man leapt from the sage to the tree, but found nothing. He froze in a crouch, looking around but seeing nothing. He stood and returned to the others and soon disappeared into the darkness.

When he was certain the warriors had gone, Eli gave the customary call of the nighthawk to tell Charlie to return to camp. As they walked into the circle of wagons, they saw several of the couples were gathered at the Tabor wagon, encouraging and comforting Audrey on the loss of her man. Zeke was standing apart, near the front of the wagon and Clara Thorne and Ted Proctor were beside him, neither talking, just being with their friend.

Eli stepped close to the group, spoke just loud enough for those close by to hear. "The Sioux came for their dead. I think they'll stay away now so I'd like to see everyone get some rest, get ready to move out at first light. If the Sioux really are gone, we can leave. If not, we need to be ready. Pass the word around, please." Most everyone nodded, moved away to go to their own wagons and make ready for the morning. Eli stepped to the back of the wagon, heard a stifled sob from within and asked, "Mrs. Tabor, we'll wait until we are gone from here to have a service for your husband. You'll have help to get him ready. Will Zeke drive the wagon for you?"

"Yes, he will. Is there any way we could find a stage or something? I'm not sure I still want to go to Montana territory without my man."

"There's none that I know of in this part of the country. There are some stage lines in Montana territory, but that's several days away. You have a good young man in Zeke, he'll take good care of you, ma'am. I'm sure you won't have to worry for anything, and the rest of us will help also."

"Thank you, Mr. McCain," mumbled the woman, readying her bed for the night. "Ask Zeke to come here, please."

"Yes'm," replied Eli, turning away, but Zeke answered, "I'm here, Ma."

Eli left the two alone, returned to his camp where Charlie had already turned in for the night. They had established a rotation of guards to keep watch for any attack, and Eli was confident they would do their job well. Bluebird had returned to the wagon of the McCoy's with her sister, Squirrel, but had left a pot of hot coffee sitting by the small fire. Eli grinned, poured himself a cup and rolled out his bedroll and sat, sipping the coffee, and muttering a silent prayer of thanksgiving to his Lord. Although they had lost two men and others were wounded, it could have been a massacre and Eli was thankful.

As the eastern horizon of low hills and flat-top mesas was shadowed by the first light of early morning, Eli stood by the trees, watching the activity of the people with the wagons. Most were getting ready to leave, few had a restful night as the plague of worry filtered through the camp. It was good to be up and moving, even in the dim light as the dark curtain retreated from the rising sun and the stars tucked themselves away in favor of the blue of the canopy above. With no sign of the Sioux, Eli got the wagons on the move, letting Charlie take the scout while he encouraged each of the wagons as they passed, then took to the backtrail alone. Bluebird was with the McCoys and her sister, enjoying the day as a family, even though it brought some painful memories to the fore. The two girls walked and scanned the terrain at the river's edge for any tasty tidbits that would complement the meals, and herbs and other plants that could prove useful for any medicinal purposes. Occasionally Bluebird would climb aboard the wagon and take a turn at driving the team, giving Max McCoy a break and time to be with his wife. She would also use the time at any opportunity to look to the backtrail to see if she could spot Eli, but he was nowhere to be seen.

The farther north they traveled, the flatter the terrain. The Big Horn basin was wide, fertile and mostly green, at least near the river, but further away, the hills and mesas seemed to flatten out as well, but the advantage was with the wagon train, easier pulling, better line of sight, and ample graze for the animals. When the captains signaled a stop for nooning, the faces showed more smiles of relief and anticipation of a good meal for their mid-day stop. The animals enjoyed the grassy flats and the shade of the cottonwoods, the children ran, laughed and played in the willows and alders, snatching random almost ripe strawberries and raspberries.

Eli took to the nearest high ground, a low butte at the edge of the dry hills west of the river. He scanned the terrain to the north, seeing a wider valley of greenery while the hills to the northwest were more of the same that had been shadowing the trail for the last many miles, rolling hills, random buttes and flat-top mesas and long plateaus. There was nothing and no one in sight that warned of danger and Eli sat back against a warm flat boulder, enjoying his time of solitude and spent some time in prayer.

Rusty was ground tied close by and Eli walked to his faithful mount, stroked his head and neck, talking to him, then stepped aboard. He reined the claybank around to start off the butte, picking his way through the big boulders that lay scattered on the hillside. The sun was warm, and the brassy sky showed bright as Eli lifted his hand to pull his hat down to shade his eyes and Rusty leaped high in the air, seemed to break in the middle and stabbed his front feet into the ground as he tried his best to kick a hole in the blue of the sky with his hind feet. Eli grabbed for the pommel, started to drive his feet into the stirrups, but they were nowhere to be had and his feet found nothing but air. He hit the end of the reins as they tore free from his grip, and he was cartwheeling head over heels down the hillside. His head bounced off the edge of a boulder, blackness washed over him, and he never felt the ground when he came to a stop. The claybank bucked his way down the hill, lunged past the still form beside the boulder, and came to a stop, every muscle in his body twitching, his nostrils flaring as he fought for air and hung his head between his spraddled front legs.

Rusty slowly lifted his head, his sides still heaving, and looked around, ears pricked and eyes wide. When he spotted the form of Eli back up the trail, he started toward him, but stopped, looking about with wide eyes and flaring nostrils. With his first buck and stab at the trail, he had smashed the head of the monstrous rattlesnake, but the air was still ripe with the smell of the serpent and Rusty was leery. The muscles in his chest, neck, and legs trembled as he searched for the snake, wary of that one or another, but the smell kept him from his friend.

IT WAS WELL after the first shadows of dusk showed that Bluebird walked into the camp of Charlie and asked, "Where is Eli? Is he not back yet?"

"Nope. Ain't seen him, but he'll be along soon I reckon," answered Charlie, reaching for the dancing coffee pot with his empty cup in hand. He looked at Bluebird, lifted his cup, "Want some?"

"No. I'm concerned about Eli. Something is wrong. He did not come in at noon, and I have not seen him since this morning. Maybe the Sioux caught up to him?"

"Nah, he's too cagey for that. He's prob'ly just lookin' things over real good. He'll be along soon, 'specially if he smells coffee on the air!" He lifted his cup to make his point.

CHAPTER 27

SEARCH

The moon was full on this cloudless night as Charlie and Bluebird rode from the camp of the wagons on the Bighorn River. With no sign of Eli and the worry of Bluebird nagging at the both of them, Charlie reluctantly agreed to accompany her on a search for Eli. When out of sight of the wagons, Charlie spoke softly, "Can you make the call of the nighthawk, you know," and he mimicked the call of the bird with the *peent peent* and a delayed deep-throated *booom.*

Bluebird grinned, nodded, "And the call of the big owl, the red-wing blackbird, yellow chat, and more."

"Eli would recognize and respond to the nighthawk, maybe the owl..." Charlie shrugged. "You take the stretch between those hills and the trail; I'll take from the trail to the river. Use a call ever so often, just in case he's hurt an' hidin'."

Bluebird nodded, nudged her mount off the trail to take to the flats, moving a little closer to the flanks of the hills. She glanced back to see Charlie also moving off the trail and toward the tree line of the river. They were about two miles down their backtrail, and Bluebird looked at the shadows that seemed to dance in the moonlight, sage, greasewood, bunch grass, an occasional juniper or piñon moving with the high-rising moon. The clatter of cicadas was interspersed with the occasional croak from bullfrogs in the backwaters of the river. The usual sounds of the night added a backdrop of harmony to the wilderness; the lonesome cry of a coyote hoping for a midnight rendezvous, the occasional howl of the desert wolf, and in the distance came the cry and scream of a cougar to be answered by another that was also looking for courtship.

Bluebird's fear was that the cougars were hunting together and had caught the scent of an injured Eli or his horse. She stood in her stirrups to search the flats, knowing if Eli was down, he would be hard to spot with the many shadows of the rocks, brush, and trees. Her hope was that Rusty, Eli's big claybank stallion was near and would be more easily seen.

The moon continued its slide across the velvet sky, making the shadows stand close and then stretch away. With the light at their backs, Bluebird and Charlie continued their search, occasionally making the call of the nighthawk, but receiving no answer. They had come just less than ten miles from the wagon camp when Bluebird spotted the point of a butte that pushed into the valley. It was a narrow stretch where the river bent to the west and the hills shouldered nearer the river. Knowing Eli's penchant for high ground and his occasional reconnoiter, she pointed her appaloosa toward the butte, cupped her hands and let loose the cry of a nighthawk. *Peent, peent,* paused and added a deep *boom.*

She stopped, leaned forward and stroked the neck of her restless mare and listened. Nothing. Standing in her stirrups, she looked to the butte, the shadows of the hill pushing toward the flat, and something moved. She snatched the Henry from the scabbard, jacked a round in and with the rifle across the pommel, she pursed her lips and made the kissing sound her appaloosa was accustomed to, and the horse stepped off with a slow walk. Guiding the horse with knee pressure, Bluebird searched the hillside, examining every shadow, watching for movement, *There!*

She was beside a big sage, the shadow masking her presence, but what she saw was near a big boulder, no more than thirty yards away and on the flank of the butte. Her appaloosa lifted her head, nostril flaring, and ears pricked, but it was not from alarm, but curiosity or interest. Bluebird smiled, leaned forward to speak to her mare.

"You smell a stallion, don't you?!"

The shadow by the boulder moved and Bluebird recognized the head of Rusty. She stood in her stirrups, cupped her hands as she looked toward the river and gave a repeated call of the nighthawk, heard an answer, and nudged her horse toward the boulder.

The two animals greeted one another with low rumbles and snorts, but Bluebird was already on the ground beside the still form of Eli. She put her head to his chest, listening for a heartbeat and breathed deep in relief when she heard a strong steady beat, but he was unconscious. After spotting the big contusion and open wound on his right forehead with dried blood covering most of his face and neck, she stretched out his legs, moved him a little to try to make him comfortable, feeling for broken bones or any other injury. His shirt was torn, his arm had a bad scrape that had bled, but she was relieved to hear him groan as she moved him.

She heard the approach of Charlie as he spoke, "Is it bad?"

"He is not awake, but he is alive. I don't know what all is hurt, his head"—she pointed to the big knot and the blood that showed black in the moonlight— "his arm, shoulder, chest and back," she shrugged. "We must get him back to the wagons where I can treat him better."

"And just how we gonna do that? You wanna make a travois?"

"No, it would be too slow and too rough. I will get on his horse, you put him behind me, tie his arms around me and you lead my horse. That would be best."

"Or we could put him in his saddle. I could ride behind him and hold him."

"But I could not lift him up to you," argued Bluebird.

Charlie grinned, nodding and turned to get Rusty set. He checked the girth and more, knowing Eli could not have loosened them so he slipped the saddle off, gave the big horse a quick rubdown, poured some water from the waterbag into his hat to give the horse a good drink, then re-rigged the big horse, ground tied him, and turned back to get Eli. Bluebird carried his feet, while Charlie had Eli under the armpits, and they made the short distance to the horse. Bluebird lowered his feet, stroked the neck of the big stallion and talked softly to him, then stepped aboard.

Charlie struggled, but slipped one of Eli's legs over the saddle skirt behind the cantle, pushed him up into the arms of Bluebird who held him steady until Charlie could use the strips of rawhide to secure the limp form of Eli. With a good but easy gait, they started for the wagons. Judging by the movement of the moon and stars, it was just shy of two hours when they neared the wagons. Charlie called out, "It's Charlie and Bluebird, comin' in with Eli."

An answer came from the last of the darkness, "Come on in!"

"We need to get him in a wagon, he's gonna need somebody with him," stated Charlie with but a glance to Bluebird.

"We will take him to your camp, a wagon is too small and does not ride easy. He should not be moved."

"But the train needs to keep movin', we can't stay here!" declared Charlie.

"I will stay with him. You take the wagons. We will follow when he is better," declared Bluebird in a tone that bode no discussion.

Charlie chuckled, shaking his head, asking himself why he even thought she would allow anyone else to tend to him. He nodded. "Alright, we'll do it your way. We might have the wagons stay here another day..."

"They must go! Get far away from the Sioux!"

"We'll get him down, get him comfortable and start tendin' to his needs, then I'll talk to the others, and *we'll* decide when we go."

As they rode to the edge of the trees and into the separate camp of the scouts, Bluebird reined up and began undoing the bonds that kept Eli close. Once he was loosed, she held on to him as Charlie lowered him to the ground. Bluebird slipped down, ran to stretch out Eli's bedroll and they lowered Eli to the blankets. Bluebird looked him over quickly, grabbed the big pot and went to the river to fetch some water, stirred up the coals and added more wood, then sat the pot at the edge of the flames.

She busied herself gathering strips of cloth for bandages and wiping rags, went to the packs to get the parfleche with the makeshift medicine bag and returned to Eli's side and began cleaning his wounds. Charlie refilled the coffeepot and sat it opposite the water pot, dropped a couple pieces of cloth into the hot water, picked them out with a stick and cautiously wrung them out, and tossed them to Bluebird. She was working feverishly and tenderly, shaking her head and searching his body for other wounds. Charlie watched and grinned, thinking about what Eli would think if he knew what she was doing.

With the coming of first light, Bluebird was able to make another once-over of Eli's body for other wounds or contusions, and nodded to Charlie, "He has many wounds and hurts, but I think he will be alright. If he would only wake up," she shook her head, looked from Charlie to Eli and sighed heavily before sitting back against the big cottonwood log that lay behind them.

"I'm gonna go talk to the others, but I'll be back shortly so you'll know what we're doin'."

"It is good," answered Bluebird, leaning back, turning to her side and stretching her arm along the log and lay her head on her arm, watching Eli, but with heavy eyes watched Charlie leave.

Chapter 28

Daylight

The bright shaft of sunlight pried its way through the squinted eyelids to give Eli an awareness of life. He closed his eyes to the pain, took a deep breath and felt more pain. A groan forced itself from his chest and he gasped for air, choked on the dust, and the movement brought more pain. He lifted his right hand to touch his head, felt a thick bandage, brought his hand before his eyes and saw a salve of some sort on his fingers. Everything beyond his hand was a blur but he detected movement, and his hand went to his hip for his holstered pistol, but there was nothing there but another poultice of salve.

"It is good to see you move. Are you hungry? Thirsty?" The questions came from a familiar voice, but he could not place it. He frowned, tried to sit up, but a soft touch to his chest brought the voice again, "Do not move. I will get what you want, if you know what you want."

Still he could not place the voice, although familiar, it

seemed to march through his memory as if lost in the wilderness.

He touched his fingers to his lips, and the voice responded, "Water?"

He dropped his hand, relaxed, and a soft hand went to the back of his neck and head, lifted and a cup touched his lips. He opened the dry parched lips, felt the water and as the precious liquid came into his mouth, he struggled to swallow, choked and spat, sought more and was able to swallow. He paused, motioned for more, and slowly emptied the cup. The soft hand lowered his head and said, "Rest. You will be good, soon. I have food and more for you when you wake."

He was propped up and being spoon-fed a hot, tasty broth when he saw the brilliant colors of sunset through the long needles of a ponderosa branch at the edge of the trees. He blinked, rubbed his eyes, and looked at the holder of the spoon. "Who are you?" asked the confused patient. Although she was familiar, he could not retrieve a name from his clouded memory.

"I am *Chosro*, Bluebird. I have been with you for many days. You were hurt three days ago, and we brought you into camp. I have been tending your wounds."

He frowned, confusion marching through his mind. "Who am I?"

Bluebird's somber expression did not change as she answered, "You are Elijah McCain. You are called Eli."

"What happened to me?"

"I believe your horse spooked at a rattlesnake. You were bucked off and fell against a big boulder. We found you much later and brought you here."

"We?"

"Your friend, Charlie, and me."

The pain in his head had become a deep, hard, ache

that caused him to hunker his head down into his neck and wince, closing his eyes as he put his hand to his head. Bluebird frowned, turned away and picked up a cup of hot tea she had prepared from the inner bark of the chokecherry, brought it to Eli's mouth and said, "This will help the pain in your head."

Eli frowned, smelled the light aroma of the tea and began to sip it as Bluebird held it for him. He was willing to do anything for relief of this pain. He finished off most of the tea and Bluebird sat the cup down, put her fingers at the back of his neck and began to slowly massage the tense muscles. Eli soon relaxed, and aided by Bluebird, lay back on his blankets and the folded blanket for a pillow and was soon asleep. Bluebird sat silently, watching, and let a slight smile come. *He will be well soon.*

The first light of early morning brought Eli awake. As was his custom, whenever he first awakened, he did not move anything, but his eyes and he searched the area before him. He spotted a stack of clothing that appeared to be his, frowned, but continued his scan. Satisfied there was no immediate danger detected, he rolled to his back, turned his head to see the blanket covered form of Bluebird and he was surprised, but not alarmed. He slowly sat up, felt the rush of pain in his head and reached up to touch the poultice and remembered he had been injured. He looked at another bandage on his arm, another on his shoulder, felt a stabbing pain in his back and realized there was another bandage there. He lifted the blankets to see a bandage on one knee, and no clothing of any kind on his body. His eyes flared, and he looked at Bluebird, but her back was to him, and she was apparently still asleep.

He slowly and quietly laid the blankets aside, crawled from the bedroll, grabbed the stack of clothing and came to his feet and quietly moved into the trees. His confusion had abated considerably. He knew who he was, who Bluebird was, and why he was here. He remembered his short flight from the hurricane deck of Rusty, his horse, and his tumbling fall and collision with the boulder. He could only assume the rest. Obviously she had tended his wounds, but the hunger he felt told him he had not eaten for some time. As he walked back into the clearing with the camp, he smelled coffee and more and his stomach turned over and reminded him it was empty. He grinned as he came near the cookfire and was a little surprised to see Bluebird was already fixing a breakfast. He smelled the coffee, looked at the pot, "Is that ready?" he asked, nodding to the pot.

Bluebird smiled, reached for the pot and poured Eli a cup of the black brew and handed it to him. He grinned, "Thanks! That smells great. And so does that," nodding to the frying pan with bacon sizzling. He saw four eggs sitting on a rock nearby, glanced to Bluebird, "Where'd you get them?"

"There was a nest in the willows near the river. You act like you're hungry—that is a good sign."

"I'm so hungry my belly button's pinchin' my backbone!" Eli chuckled. "So, Bluebird, you say we've been here three days?"

She nodded, and he continued, "And they've been gone those three days?"

"No, they left the day after we brought you in."

"Two days, hmmm."

She nodded again as she tended the bacon. As each piece was finished cooking, she forked it to a tin plate, and when the pan was empty of bacon, she cracked an egg, poured it into the pan and as it sizzled and popped, she quickly added another. He watched as she carefully slid the eggs to the edge of the pan and slowly rolled them over on themselves. When she was satisfied, she lifted the pan from the hot coals and slipped the eggs onto the tin plate and handed it to Eli.

He grinned broadly, took a deep breath, closed his eyes and dropped his head and said a short prayer of thanksgiving to the Lord, loud enough to be heard by Bluebird, and at the "Amen" he began devouring the breakfast. As he ate, Bluebird prepared herself a similar breakfast, and sat beside Eli to work on her own.

As she ate, Eli asked, "So, it's just been you and me for the past two days, now goin' on three?"

"Yes," she responded between bites.

"So, who took off my clothes?"

"I did," she giggled. "But since we are joined, and you are my husband, it is alright." She smiled and continued eating.

Eli frowned, "Now wait a minute!" choking on his food. Wide-eyed, he looked up at her, "I know my memory ain't perfect, but I'd surely remember somethin' like that! You mean to say we are married—man and wife!?"

She smiled broadly, nodding, and continuing to eat. When she paused her eating, "They said you would not think it right for us to be together and for me to do what was needed, if we were not husband and wife. So, the man you call Parson, opened his book, spoke some words, and said we were married!" She had a stoic expression and Eli was flabbergasted.

"They can't do that!" he declared. "Not when a man's unconscious, they can't!"

"But you have no reason to be shamed. We are joined. The parson said," she responded, before taking another big bite of eggs and bacon.

"Now, why can I remember ever'thin' else and not remember that?!"

"It is easy to remember things that hurt, but what is good if not as easy to remember," philosophized Bluebird, rising to finish the breakfast doin's. When her back was to Eli, she smiled broadly and went about her work without saying anymore. She called over her shoulder as she started to the water to wash the utensils, "It happens among my people often," and stifled a giggle.

CHAPTER 29

REUNITED

The Bighorn River made a dog-leg bend to the east to make its lazy way around a long finger of land before the confluence with the Nowood River. There was timber on the point of the peninsula, good grass on most of the piece of land. Beyond the river to the east, low rolling sandhills stood proudly with their sage, cacti, and rabbit brush with scattered patches of dry bunch grass, while to the west across the three mile wide valley, rolled low hills with dust devils dancing all about. Charlie stopped the wagons, directed them onto the peninsula with, "We'll make camp here tonight. Come mornin', maybe give the parson an opportunity for his preachin' and' singin'."

Ted Proctor sat his mount beside Charlie, leaning on the pommel of his saddle and looked sidelong at Charlie. "You plannin' on stoppin' a while and wait fer Eli an' Bluebird?"

Charlie looked at him, "Dunno, thot' about it, but..." he shrugged. He turned back to watch the wagons pass. "He got hurt purty bad, might take a while for him to get where he can ride. I don't wanna go on without him, but these folks are anxious to get to the goldfields and Virginia City. The way some of 'em think is that every day we spend on the trail is one day less for them to pan for gold or whatever they have their minds set on."

"Ummhmmm," answered Ted. "That's what Pa says. He thinks somebody else will get all the gold 'fore we get there, but Ma, she just wants to get a house built 'fore winter sets in."

"Smart woman," answered Charlie, waving to Squirrel who was sitting beside Max McCoy on the driver's seat of their wagon as they passed. The girl waved to Ted, then stood on the seat to look back to see if she could see Eli and Bluebird. But there was nothing but dust following the wagons.

The trail onto the peninsula dropped off the shoulder of flatland where eons ago the river had carved its path through the land, leaving the meandering river in a sandy-bottomed stretch of old river beds where the confused river always sought the easiest passage. As they made their way to the stretch of river bottom soil, the farmers noticed the fertility of the land, the hunters watched for game for fresh meat, and the gold fever crowd looked longingly at the water and the geography of the nearby land. Charlie just looked for a shady place to make his camp and have a little privacy, which he found under a cluster of tall cottonwoods and scattered chokecherry bushes and random strawberry and raspberry patches.

He had built a small fire, just big enough for his coffee pot, and was pouring a cup of steaming java when the two captains walked into his camp and Nolan Ryan asked, "Can we talk to you Charlie?"

"Sure. Want some coffee?" he asked, nodding to the pot.

"Nah, we won't take much time. Our womenfolk are fixin' our supper." He paused, stubbed his toe in the dirt and looked to Charlie who had seated himself on a downed, grey cottonwood log. "We was wonderin' how long we're gonna be here."

"You mean here at this camp?" At their nod he continued. "What'chu got in mind?"

"Well, we're anxious to get to the gold fields, but our women didn't get much of a chance to catch up on the wash an' such back there where the Sioux hit us, an' we had to leave, sudden like, and with Eli still missin', we was thinkin' 'bout stayin' at least an extry day here." His statement was more of a question as he looked askance to Charlie.

Charlie chuckled. "Uh, ain't I workin' for you folks?"

"Yeah, but..." Nolan shrugged.

"Then as long as it don't put us in danger, I reckon it'd be alright to stay. Not too far away we got us a dry stretch to cross, so the rest would prob'ly be good for the animals."

Both men grinned, showed relief on their faces and Nolan nodded. "Good, good. Then we'll pass the word!"

"You do that," agreed Charlie, and poured a refill of coffee, grinning himself and sitting back on the log, elbows on his knees and thinking about his friend.

———

ELI STOOD, looking at the retreating form of Bluebird, and went to the horses. He brought them into the camp, tethered them, and began readying them for travel. He started with Rusty and began giving him a good brush-

ing, ridding his coat of dirt and burs that he had accumu-
lated in his graze of the area and rolling in the dirt. He
did the same with Grey and as he finished, he saw Bluebird returning and she asked, "What are you doing?"

"Gettin' the horses ready to travel, what's it look
like?"

"You should rest another day, you're not well," she
pleaded.

"We need to catch up to the wagons 'fore they get too
far ahead. If we get started, I figger we can catch up to
'em in a couple days."

She put on a stern expression. "But if you get tired,
will we stop?"

"We'll stop when I think I can't make it any further.
But right now, after that good breakfast, I'm ready for
just about anything!" he declared, reaching under the
belly of Rusty to grab the latigo. When he glanced back
at Bluebird she was smiling broadly and asked, "Anything?" with a coy and mischievous look on her face.

Eli grunted as he pulled the latigo tight and wrapped
the strap tight below the "D" ring and refused to look at
the woman, but slowly shook his head as if he did not
hear what she said.

She laughed a little, took the pans and utensils to the
panniers and packed them away, just as Eli finished with
the packsaddle and prepared to lift the panniers to the
rack. When he finished, he helped Bluebird with her
saddle and packs and the sun had barely cleared the
eastern horizon and they were on their way.

As usual, Eli had packed the shotgun on the packhorse, but kept his Winchester in a scabbard under the
right fender, butt to the back, and the Spencer in a scabbard that hung off the pommel on the left, butt forward.
He glanced at Bluebird to see she had put her Henry in

the new scabbard like he carried the Winchester, but her quiver of arrows and unstrung bow were at her back.

They followed the wagon trail known as Bridger Trail, that kept to the west of the river, oftentimes crowded against the hills and buttes that occasionally pushed into the valley and near the waterway. True to his word, Eli did not push the horses, giving them their head and letting them settle into a comfortable gait. Water and shade were always near, and they made good time, but Eli's weakness combined with his returning hunger, began to wear on him and was noticed by Bluebird. She stood in her stirrups and pointed to a break in the trees at the river and said, "There, that would be a good place!"

"A good place for what?" asked Eli, straightening up to sit tall in the saddle.

"A good place to find a turkey or some ducks for a good meal. You are weak and need a good meal. It won't take too long, and the horses won't mind getting a rest." She nudged her appaloosa toward the break and turned to motion him to follow. "C'mon!" she called, grinning and allowing no argument.

She had stopped at a spacious clearing with tall grass and close trees that afforded cover as well as a break from the rising wind. She dropped to the ground, looked back at Eli as she stripped the quiver from her back to string her bow, and instructed, "You strip the horses, I'll get us some food!" With a broad smile, she nocked an arrow and started through the trees toward a backwater of the river. She had heard the low gobble of a turkey and thought it would make just such a meal.

Eli took a deep breath, stepped down and began stripping the gear from the horses, allowing each in turn a good roll in the dirt, then led them to water. As they came to the edge of the river, Bluebird was already returning with a big turkey and two ducks.

She was smiling broadly, "We're going to eat good this time!" she declared, and walked back to the clearing.

Eli watched the woman, shaking his head, but enjoying watching her walk away and he grinned, still wondering about the "wedding" she had told about. He thought Charlie might have been up to his tricks, but he couldn't believe that the parson would willingly be a part of such a stunt. So if the parson was involved, maybe she was right, and they had been "married." He shook his head, and followed her back to the clearing to help with the cookfire. They might be here a while, although he was feeling somewhat weak, and not willing to take unnecessary risks.

CHAPTER 30

RETURN

They had made good time, and after the sumptuous meal of turkey and a few hours rest, Eli was anxious to get back on the trail. He knew Charlie was more than capable, but he had given his word to the people, and he wanted to see it through. As they rode from their camp by the river, he glanced to the sky and knew the sun would soon be resting on the western horizon, and with dusk coming, they would have maybe two to three hours of daylight, but he was also counting on the full moon. Last night, the moon was waning from full, but if the night sky was clear, the three-quarter moon and the stars would provide ample light for them to continue their journey.

They had ridden until just past midnight and at Bluebird's insistence, they stopped to rest the horses and themselves. And now, with the rising sun off their right shoulder, they resumed their travel on the Bridger Trail. There was ample sign of the recent passing of the wagons, and Eli was encouraged at the freshness of the sign. He glanced to Bluebird "We're gettin' close, might catch up with 'em later today. Those horse apples are fresh, so they can't be too far ahead."

Bluebird grinned, "I saw that...those"—pointing to the freshest droppings from the teams— "were made yesterday, late, so they are not too far away."

The trail hugged the flanks of the low hills on the west side of the Bighorn basin and occasionally the untamed Bighorn River pushed closer to the hills, but the narrow neck of land they traversed was about a third of a mile wide as compared to most of the basin with the river giving way at least a mile on either side. They stopped for the nooning, and Bluebird broiled the last duck over the small cookfire. They were in the trees along the west river bank and the minimal smoke from the dry wood fire would be filtered by the overhanging branches of the cottonwoods. Eli stretched out, his head on a folded blanket and his hat over his eyes, and within moments, he was snoring and snorting, making Bluebird grin at his noisy sleeping, but she was glad to see him resting. She had noticed how easily he tired, but his stubbornness would not allow them to stop. She resolved to let him sleep however long he would.

They had stopped at another narrow neck of land where the river made a dog-leg bend and pointed east, but in the bend there was pie shaped island and in the shallow water on the near bank, Bluebird heard some more ducks and looked at Eli, who had awakened at the smell of dinner, and she asked, "There are more ducks, there," pointing to the river. "Would you like me to get some more?"

Eli grinned, shook his head, "Nah, I'm thinkin' I'd like somethin' more fillin', like buffalo or elk or some-thin' like that. But..." Eli paused, grinning, "If there's some eggs..." He shrugged.

She jumped to her feet and grabbed a leather pouch she had used before and slipped away through the trees while Eli made short work of the rest of the broiled duck. She was back with a broad smile, hoisted the leather pouch, and it was easy to see the bulging pouch had eggs within.

"You better be careful, you might break 'em!" cautioned Eli.

Bluebird insisted on checking his wounds and bandages, applied more of her Balm of Gilead and a salve made from sage and milkweed, and fresh bandages, paying closer attention to the wound on his head. But she smiled as she finished her nursing, and nodded, but she was hesitant to move away from him. They were soon on their way and Eli glanced to the sun, back to Bluebird, "How long did you let me sleep?"

"Two hands," she answered, grinning.

"Two hours? You shoulda woke me up!" He turned in his saddle to look at the sun that was lowering in the western sky, held his hand out at arm's length, and by stacking his hands one over the other, he knew each finger was worth fifteen minutes, and as he measured, "Let's see, four hands, four hours, that'd be 'bout six, another hour of dusk, to seven, yeah, I bet we find 'em 'fore full dark!" he declared, grinning.

They saw the river had made a general bend to the northwest and Eli knew it would not be too far until they would leave the river valley and move across the bend of dry land to the Greybull River. Hopefully they would find the wagons before that fork with Elk Creek that marked the way.

"There!" stated Bluebird, pointing to the tracks of the many wagons that turned off the trail and dropped over the lip of the flat to go to the river bottom. With a check of the sign, she added, "They did not come back this way. They are either there beyond the trees, or they left a different way."

Eli stood in his stirrups, let a smile split his face as he said, "Nope! They're still there! I can see some white wagon bonnets!" pointing to the peninsula at the bend of the river.

———

THEY WERE WARMLY GREETED by the lookouts and by the families as they rode into the circle of wagons. Eli asked for Charlie's camp, and as Bluebird nodded toward the McCoy wagon, he started toward the trees and Charlie's camp. As he rode into the clearing, he was not surprised to see Charlie come to his feet, wiping the sleep from his eyes and grinning at Eli. "Well, din't think I'd wake up an' see you! I am awake, ain't I? You doin' alright?"

Eli chuckled, stepped down and said, "I will be after we talk a little." He glanced to the cookfire, saw the coffeepot sitting on a rock nearby, "Any coffee left?"

"Nah, but I'll get some goin', then we can talk," answered Charlie, grabbing up the pot to get more water. He called over his shoulder, "There's a little spring hyar that's mighty sweet!" He quickly returned, sat the pot near the coals, put a couple pieces of wood on and sat back on the log, looking at his friend. "You do look better than the last time I saw you, but you ain't as purty as you used to be, that's fer certain!"

Eli chuckled, and shook his head. "I seem to remember somethin' concerning the parson. Did he come by our camp while I was out?"

"Ummhmmm," answered a grinning Charlie. "But you was out, that's fer certain."

"And was Bluebird there?"

"Ummhmm, she wouldn't leave your side, nohow, noway!" He chuckled.

"What'd the parson do?"

"Oh he prayed, said a few words, and left."

"Anything special?"

Charlie frowned. "Whatchu mean, 'special'? You wouldn't know anyhow, you was not even movin' or moanin'." Charlie chuckled. "Why? You thinkin' some-thin' happened?" He turned his head away to stifle a laugh.

"Oh, I dunno. Bluebird has this crazy notion that the parson married us while I was out and now she thinks we're husband and wife!"

Charlie busted out in a big laugh that caused him to fall backward off the cottonwood log. He scrambled up, dusting himself off, all the while laughing and grinning. "Told you!"

"What'd you tell me?" asked Eli, frowning and wondering what else he might have forgotten.

"I told you she wanted to be yore woman! She was bound an' determined!" Charlie laughed, looked up to see Bluebird walking across the open to their camp, "An' lookee thar, here comes Missus McCain!" Mebbe I better give you two some privacy, what say?"

Eli frowned and pointed to the log. "You stay right there, buster, don't you even think about leavin'!" he growled.

And it wasn't just Bluebird, Violet McCoy and Squirrel were right behind her as they walked into the little clearing. Bluebird walked over to Eli, reached for the bandage on his head, "I need to change that, you're starting to bleed again." She pointed to the log and started for the panniers that were still aboard Grey and she turned and looked back at Eli. "You have not taken off his packs? Why?"

"Been talkin' to this rascal!" growled Eli.

Bluebird smiled at Charlie, nodded and turned back to Eli. With the medicine bag in hand, she pointed to the log, and he dropped his head and seated himself beside Charlie. Squirrel came close and with a somber expression on her face, asked, "How is my brother?"

Eli looked up at her. "Brother?"

Squirrel looked surprised until Violet McCoy came close, smiled, and explained, "Why yes, of course, Eli. She is Bluebird's sister, and now you are her brother!" She clasped her hands together, smiled broadly, "I'm so happy for the both of you!" She looked at Squirrel. "Come Squirrel, we have work to do. They will come to our wagon for supper, and we must be ready."

Eli watched them go, looked at Charlie and Bluebird, and breathed heavily as she tended the wounds and when she finished, he asked, "We're going to the McCoy's for supper?"

Bluebird nodded. "Yes, they asked, and I said we would be happy to eat with them. Charlie is to come also." She flashed her smile and turned to put away the medicinals, glanced to a grinning Charlie and winked.

———

AS THEY WALKED into the circle, many of the folks greeted Eli and Bluebird, some expressing their gladness at their return, some just smiling and waving. Eli shook his head as they neared the wagon and was pleased to see a good size makeshift table and the parson standing near the wagon. Eli nodded and greeted everyone, took the offered seat with the parson on one side and Bluebird on the other. It was a fine meal prepared by the ladies, and after it was all done and they sat drinking coffee and talking, Eli looked at the parson and began, "Parson, I vaguely remember hearing you when they brought me in from the hills, just what was it you said?"

The parson frowned and answered, "Well Eli, what I usually do at times like that is I read a portion of scripture, and I did that. I read from Psalm 91, beginning with verse 9 to the end of the chapter. Then I prayed for you and Bluebird, and she asked a couple questions, I don't remember what all they were, but then I left."

"Uh, when you prayed for me'n Bluebird, was it anything special, you know, for any special purpose?"

The parson frowned, glanced to see Bluebird grinning and holding her hand to her mouth to keep from laughing, and a glance around the table showed others doing much the same. He looked at Eli and asked, "Uh, what purpose would you be referring to?"

"You know, like marriage!?"

And at that, no one could keep from laughing and Charlie explained, "Parson, Bluebird told him you married 'em while he was unconscious and that they were now husband and wife!"

That brought more laughter from most everyone but Eli, who sat, shaking his head and gritting his teeth as he looked from Charlie to Bluebird. "And all of you were in on it!?" As he looked around the table there was a mix of expressions from some nodding their confessions, to others shaking their heads but grinning and laughing. He looked at the parson who was also laughing, but Eli's expression prompted the Parson to explain. "No, I was not 'in on it', but you have to admit, it is kinda funny.

Especially when you know that Psalm 91 speaks about *he hath set his love upon me, therefore will I deliver him:* and it goes on to say *I will be with him in trouble, I will deliver him and honor him,* that does kinda talk about Bluebird's care for you during that time." He chuckled, glancing from Eli to Bluebird.

Eli turned to look at a smiling and laughing Bluebird and squinted his eyes and said, "And you! I prob'ly oughta take you out yonder and give you the spanking you deserve!"

Charlie laughed and looked at the parson, "Maybe you did marry 'em, parson. He's sure actin' like a husband!" which brought more laughter around the table.

CHAPTER 31

MOVING

The animals were rested and eager to be on the move. The clothes had been washed, the men fed, the youngsters anxious, and the women happy, when the train pulled out of camp with the grey light of early morning chasing them from their place of rest. They put the confluence of Nowood River and Bighorn River behind them and started for the bench of dry land as they headed northwest away from the rising sun.

They crossed the fertile valley, bumped over a dry creek bed and took the trail west that followed the creek bed and flanked the rising hills. It was a clear day, although Eli had spotted some distant threatening clouds far to the west, and the rising sun shone bright on their backs. The dusty trail forced drivers and riders to lift their neckerchiefs over their faces and the horses and mules to snort and blow dust from their nostrils as they tromped westward. When the creek bed pushed against the flank of the hills, the trail bent more northward to leave the creek bed and followed the cut between buttes, rose over an alkali and acidic soil showing white and pink that appeared as a blanket of color over the dry land.

The trail dropped into a wide draw with another dry creek bed cutting the trail and turning the train northwest. It was late afternoon when Eli and Bluebird broke from the hills into a grassy and fertile valley that carried a meandering river from the west bound for the east and a confluence with the Bighorn. "That'd be the Greybull River," stated Eli, nodding to the willow and cottonwood lined waterway.

"My people call it *tosapitteh poitsanteh* which is white buffalo, the sacred animal of my people."

Eli lifted his shaded eyes to the lowering sun, but it had tucked itself behind some dark clouds in the west. He stood in his stirrups and looked to the river below, the hills behind them, and the darkening clouds. "It's been a long day, maybe we should camp here, cross in the mornin'," he drawled, glancing to Bluebird.

Bluebird just pointed to the west, "Those are storm clouds, they're already watering the hills there, and if it comes this way, all the water from the mountain storm will come with it. Perhaps we should cross *before* the storm comes."

Eli stood in his stirrups again, looked to the western hills and saw the wispy curtain of rain coming from the black-bottomed clouds. He slowly nodded his head, "Ummhmm, that's the kinda storm that could flood the plains." He looked across the valley of the Greybull and knew the trail would follow the river west before turning more northward, but if there was a good campsite on the north side, it might be best to push on across, even though the animals and the people would be tired.

"The water is already showing muddy and rising," observed Bluebird.

"You go down to the river, check the crossing. I'll go back and hurry 'em up a mite, make sure we get across 'fore it's too late!" He pulled Rusty's head around and dug heels to his ribs to take off back down the trail to meet the wagons. It was just a short jaunt and he pulled up alongside the lead wagon, driven by Oleg Hansen, sided by his wife Grace with the young daughter Cecilia standing beside her mother and waving at Eli. He grinned, told Oleg, "We need to pick up the pace, there's a river crossing, more of a creek really, but we need to get across 'fore that storm"— nodding to the western clouds— "hits and makes the water too high."

"Ja, Ja, I can do dat!" declared the grinning Swede. He slapped the reins to the butts of his mules and their heads came up and they started off at a slow trot.

Eli waited for the next wagon, said the same thing to each one as they passed and as the last wagon, driven by Jim Dillon, who had been wounded when the Sioux had attacked, but was mending well, "You need to stay close behind the wagon in front of you, we need to get across the river 'fore the storm gets us!" Jim nodded, cracked the bullwhip over the heads of his horses and they leaned into their traces and pushed close behind the other wagons.

Satisfied with the driver's work and efforts, Eli looked back to see if he could see Charlie and within moments, his friend pulled up alongside. Eli motioned for them to get to moving and they rode together, taking the low flanks to the west of the trail and passed the long string of wagons, arriving at the river just as the lead wagon of Oleg Hansen pushed on across.

Charlie asked, "So, what's all the hurryin' about? That ain't much more'n a crick!"

Eli lifted his shoulders, arched his back, showing the strain of the ride. He pointed to the west. "That!"

Charlie looked, saw a distant stab of blue-white lightning and waited, listening. He counted slowly, waited, and when he hit thirty, the rumble of thunder could easily be heard. He looked at Eli. "That ain't but 'bout six mile away!"

Eli nodded. "Let's get 'em movin'. That crossing could take 'em side by side."

The two men worked quickly, motioning the wagons to take the crossing, staggered but closer than in a single line, making the crossing a little easier. It was a shallow creek and a good wide flat rock bottom. He shook his head when he saw several of the gold-hungry men leaning over to look at the creek bottom, even though the water was already showing muddy, they hoped to see the glimmer of riches but were disappointed. When Arne Pedersen leaned over to look long and hard, stopping his wagon, Parson Shadrach Spencer barked at him, "Git that wagon movin' fool! The storm's comin' and the crick's risin'!"

Arne looked wide-eyed at the usually quiet and reserved parson, nodded, and answered with a wave and a slap of the reins to the backsides of his horses. The wagon jerked and the horses took to the low-rising bank and the Pedersen wagon was soon sided by the parson's. Parson Spencer, looking a little sheepish. "Sorry Arne, didn't mean to bark, but..." He shrugged, and Arne grinned as they both kept their wagons moving away from the river toward the selected campsite where the wagons were circling up near the flanks of the low-rising sagebrush covered buttes.

The cool air of the coming storm slapped Eli's face, prompting him to look to the west and see what he had thought was a small rainstorm had grown into a sure-fire thunderstorm of churning black clouds, crooked lances of stabbing lightning and the continuous roll and rumble of thunder that seemed to shake the branches of the trees and make the animals tremble. He looked at the wagons, guessed that about half, maybe more had crossed and the last of the trader's wagons were climbing the bank on the far side. He counted the remaining wagons, *ten more!* And a glance to the storm made him shake his head and holler to be heard over the thunder. "Move it! Git across and hurry! Floodwaters comin'!"

He rode back along the line of wagons, shouted the same thing and saw several of the wagons push up beside the one before them, crowding their way to the crossing.

Jerry Proctor hollered to his son, "Ted! Get on yore horse and git on acrost!"

Ted nodded, jumped off the back of the wagon, swung aboard his bareback grey gelding, grabbed a handful of mane and dug heels to cross the creek upstream of the wagons. The wagons behind them saw Ted take his horse.

Fritz Bondurant hollered to his twelve-year-old son, "Daniel, take your sister, Adelaide, take the horse and get on across!"

He was quickly answered by his son, "Sure Pa! We can do that!"

They were followed by the two sons of the Dillon wagon behind them, a big bay ridden by eleven-year-old Louis, and his nine-year-old brother, Edwin.

The rain and wind came with the rolling thunder that echoed across the narrow valley of the Greybull River.

The trees with their new spring fresh leaves, bent and waved with the wind, the rain, drops as big as a man's thumb, came with a fury and pelted the horses, wagon bonnets, and people that shaded their eyes and faces, ducked their heads from the wind, and struggled on to cross the river while those on the far side, pushed toward the lee side of the hills where the others were making camp. They would find no dry wood for fires, and it would be a cold camp tonight.

Charlie and Eli had already crossed the river and sat their saddles on the far bank beside Bluebird, watching the wagons cross, and from their high ground, Eli kept looking upstream, fearful of floodwaters. He turned to see the last two wagons, on the downstream side, and slightly ahead was the Bondurant wagon, and the last wagon was driven by the determined Jim Dillon, his wife close to his side, her arm around his back, both with heads ducked and necks bent against the wind.

The roar that caught Eli's attention was unmistakable, he knew floodwaters were coming, but he was hoping it would not be too bad, this was not a big river, and the banks were not steep. But the floodwaters came crashing with a foaming and raging headwater that paid no attention to the riverbanks and pushed its way through the cottonwoods, alders, aspen and scattered pines, Every living thing bowed to its onslaught and when Eli, Bluebird and Charlie spotted the monstrous wave, they wheeled their mounts around and slapped legs to escape the onslaught. Eli looked over his shoulder to see the Bondurant wagon climbing from the riverbed, the floodwaters already crashing against the big rear wheels, but the Dillon wagon was pushed away, the wall of water, foam, and debris included an uprooted tree whose tangled roots and branches seemed to reach out and grab the wagon, tilting it to the side, and it began to upset and with a scream from Emma, wagon and horses were toppled into the floodwaters.

"Oh my gawd!" came a screaming voice from the Bondurant wagon, the last wagon across. Both Fritz and Emily stood on the driver's seat of their wagon, looking back at the disappearing Dillon wagon.

Eli hollered at Fritz, "Get that wagon movin'! It could still rise and come up here!" As he hollered, he and Charlie and Bluebird slapped legs to their mounts to retreat from the monster created by the thunderstorm that still lingered overhead.

CHAPTER 32

VISITOR

After the scare and tragedy of the crossing of the Greybull River, the travelers were relieved that the only water crossings for the next three days were small creeks and dry washes. They continually moved north across the flats with the occasional rolling hills and an abundance of sage, cacti, jackrabbits, and coyotes. Of an evening, the two young hunters, Zeke and Tom always took time in the dusk of the day to hunt for meat and were mostly successful.

Things began to show a little more green mid-day on the fourth day north of the Greybull crossing as the trail sided the wandering and twisting Whistle Creek. But when the creek turned east, and the trail pointed north, they soon dropped off the flat plateau and dropped into the valley of the Shoshone. But the Shoshone River was an easy crossing, although the hearts beat a little quicker and the drivers stood in front of their seats, nervously watching the water's depth. Once across, they made a quick stop for the nooning, giving the animals rest and water, but the further north they traveled, the more anxious everyone became to get to the gold fields and the end of the journey.

It was still late spring, and most everything was showing at least a hint of green. The land that would later show colors of buff, grey, tan, and brown, showed more life at this time of year, especially after the recent rains. The sky was a brilliant blue, clouds were few and the air was cool, all making for pleasant travel. As dusk made its slow approach, Eli directed the wagons to circle up near the chuckling waters of what they would later learn was Polecat Creek. It was clear, gurgling fresh water, and folks replenished their water barrels, some of the women washed clothes by the dim light of dusk, and surprisingly, several folks, both men and women, in separate pools of course, took much needed baths. It was a refreshing stop, and Eli passed the word around, they would make an early start in the morning.

———

A GOOD DAY'S travel brought them into Montana Territory, the trail sided Sage Creek and they stopped for the night at the confluence of Sage and Piney creeks, appropriately named since Sage originated in land covered with sage and Piney came from the mountains that lay to the east and showed the travelers the first black timber and blue hills in Montana Territory. West of their camp an abundance of dusty mesas and round topped buttes marched northward with the trail.

It was another comfortable camp, and Charlie and Eli found a private cove of the creek where the trout were jumping and snatching a hatch of mayflies and tempting the men to have fish for supper. Bluebird offered, "If you want fish, you catch, I fix, we eat!" she declared smiling.

The men were agreeable, helped Bluebird with the panniers that held the pots and pans, started her cook-fire, and walked to the creek. The men had fishing lines and hooks, caught some grasshoppers and began their fishing.

When the smiling men walked back into camp with a stringer of cutthroat and rainbow trout, Bluebird explained, "You clean, I cook!" and smiled at the men as she shoveled some coals atop the dutch oven that held some biscuits and cornmeal. A pot was bubbling on the grill with fresh cut cattail shoots, yampa root, and pota-toes. She rolled the trout in cornmeal, slid it into the frying pan and they soon had a sumptuous meal unlike any they had so far. The satisfied men sat back, hot coffee in hand and looked at Bluebird as she busied herself cleaning up. Charlie looked at Eli and when Bluebird was out of earshot, he asked, "You gonna marry that girl, or not?"

Eli chuckled, glanced to where Bluebird was packing away the utensils, and dropped his eyes to the fire and quietly answered, "Thought about it."

"I think you'd make her a mighty happy woman if you did!" responded Charlie. "Then you could come see me'n Meaghan an' our new young'un."

"Come see you? You don't even know where you're gonna be livin' yet!" declared a chuckling Eli. The men talked a while, Bluebird sat with them a while, and she rose to go to the McCoy wagon where she and her sister stayed together. Eli stood, walked a short ways with her and held her hand as they walked. When away from the camp and the wagons, he asked, "Have you and Squirrel thought much about what you'll do after the wagons get to the end of the trail?"

"We've talked a little, but have not decided. My

mother had a sister with the *Agaideka* band in the north near Three Rivers, but…" she shrugged, keeping her eyes down. In many ways, she had let Eli know how she felt and hoped to be joined with him, but he had not spoken of it with her.

He began with, "Have you thought about finding a mate, you know, taking a husband?"

She cocked her head to the side, looked at him and frowned, shook her head and walked away without answering. Eli stood watching, knowing he had failed in his attempt to talk, but he still was not certain of his feelings and his plans for the future, but every time he gave it any thought, she was at the forefront of his mind. When he spent time with his Lord, he sought an answer, a direction, but he just was not sure. He enjoyed being with her, thrilled at the sight of her, missed her when they were apart, but his experience at what most folks call love was a bit limited. He had been married, but that was more of a promise to a friend to take care of his wife and children, than a marriage of love. He had met other women, and some had expressed their interest in marriage, he thought of Constance Wellington, the woman he met on the riverboat on his way to Montana the first time, she was beautiful, a successful business woman, and interested. And the Piikani Blackfoot woman, Morning Dove, she told him she wanted to be joined with him, but that was not at a good time. And of course, there was Donna Kennedy, who he found in the woods and helped her buy a café in Walla Walla, she hoped to become his wife. But all those were during his search for his boys, and he was not willing to stop his search. But now…he shrugged and turned back to their camp.

Charlie greeted him with a grin. "So, did you ask her?"

Eli frowned. "Ask her what?"

"You know, to get married!"

Eli shook his head, grabbed a stick and threw it at a laughing Charlie, who ducked and rolled away.

They turned in for the night, their horses tethered nearby, and as always, the men were a little isolated from the wagons, and they slept lightly, always attentive to their horses for any possible danger. As Eli and Charlie lay in their blankets, small talk continued as Charlie asked, "Did you see that colt that Clara's sorrel foaled? It's a purty one, flaxen mane and tail, dark chestnut color, stud. He's gonna make a mighty fine horse one day."

Eli chuckled, "That black mare of Sheridan's is due to drop any day, hope she gets it done so we don't have to split the wagons, you know, some'd want to stay with the Sheridans, other'sd want to keep goin'."

"Yeah, some o' them gold-hungry wanna be miners can be downright callous about just about anything that keeps 'em from gettin' to the gold country. Sometimes I'd like to just tell 'em to take off on their own, see if they can find their way without gettin' scalped or somethin'," grumbled Charlie. "Oh well, let's get some sleep."

———

IT WAS the nervous stomping of Rusty that brought Eli instantly awake. He quickly searched the surrounding area before coming from his blankets, but when he did he had the Spencer in hand. Charlie slipped from his blankets, pulled on his moccasins and stood beside Eli. Neither speaking, both standing in the night shade of the spruce at the edge of their camp, looking toward the wagons, when they saw a small figure coming toward them at a run. They recognized the form of Bluebird just as she broke from the sage and Eli asked, "What is it?"

"Grizzly! Big boar, going after the horses!" he declared, pointing to the rope corral corner of the camp beside the alders of the creek.

The men took off at a run toward the remuda, hearing the ruckus of panicked horses and mules, the growl of a bear and the scream of a frightened mare. A gunshot pierced the black of night, a scream from a woman followed, followed by another scream and gunshot.

Eli and Charlie came to an abrupt halt when they saw the big grizzly come to his back feet, pawing at the air with his forefeet, and cock his head to the side and let out a thunderous roar that seemed to rattle the bonnets of the wagons. People were running, shouting, screaming, and the horses and mules had broken the rope corral and were stampeding through the middle of the wagons. Eli stopped, lifted the Spencer, brought it to full cock and fired. The muzzle flash stabbed at the dark, the bullet flew true, but the big boar just turned to face to this new threat. The grizz dropped to all fours and with a roar and a twist of his head and a snap of his jaws that caused bloody slobbers to fly around his head, he charged the two men.

Charlie fired, jacked another round, fired again, and dust rose from the mottled coat of the silvertip grizz, but his charge was not stayed. Eli had fired two more rounds from the big Spencer, but the boar only slightly stumbled, but kept coming. Both men fired, Charlie at the neck and chest of the big beast, Eli at the open mouth and head. All of the bullets struck the beast, and he dropped to his belly and slid to a stop within two feet of the men who kept their rifles trained on the now still form.

The men did not move, willingly at least, although both showed a slight tremble and gasped a ragged breath. They looked at one another, shook their heads and stepped to the side of the mountain monster and poked the carcass with the muzzles of their rifles, but the grizzly was dead. Eli looked at Charlie.

"We better make a circle of the camp, see if there are any others. Sometimes these things travel together."

Charlie said, "Let's check to see if that thing kilt anythin'."

Eli answered, "You go ahead, then make the rounds. I'll start thisaway."

Charlie nodded, pointed with his rifle to the right edge of the wagons, and started off as Eli went the opposite way. The camp had quieted from the pandemonium, but everyone was still wide awake, looking about and talking.

As Eli neared the Proctor wagon, Jerry asked, "He dead?"

"Yup. Charlie's checkin' the remuda, most have run off, but that's what the bear was after. Don't know if he killed anything, but Charlie's checkin'."

"How we gonna get the horses back?" asked Jerry, frowning and running his hands through his disheveled hair.

"Some of us still have ours, kept 'em tethered at the wagons and such, so we'll see, come morning."

The two men made the circle of the wagons and Charlie reported, "Looks like the only thing he got was what he smelled that brought him close. That black mare of Sheridan's was birthing her colt. The grizz kilt both the mare and the colt." He shook his head at the report, and added, "Least he didn't get any o' the kids and such."

"Ummhmm," agreed Eli. "But we have a roundup to take care of tomorrow, and we'll need to tote that grizz away. His smell will keep any of the horses and mules from comin' back."

"Then let's get some o' the men busy diggin' a hole or somethin'," suggested Charlie.

CHAPTER 33

NORTHWEST

When Eli and Charlie returned to the carcass of the bear, they were surprised to see Bluebird and Squirrel already at work skinning the beast. She saw them approach, smiled, and continued her work. Eli frowned, "What're you doing? We were gonna have the men dig a hole and bury that thing. With its smell still around, the horses won't come back!"

"I know. But this is a good coat and will make a fine trophy. His claws and teeth will make a necklace for my man to wear and show he is a great hunter! We"— glancing to her sister— "will take the hide and begin the work of tanning. The horses will not smell the bear, the hide will be underwater, and you should tell all the men to relieve themselves, you know"—and she motioned to his crotch— "in the water where the hide will be. We will do the same. It will make the tanning easier and take away the smell of the bear."

Eli looked at Charlie, back to Bluebird, shook his head and started back to the camp. Charlie followed, chuckling. He asked, "Din't you know that? I mean, about the urine being used as part of the tanning process?"

"I knew it, but..." He shook his head and continued walking. He paused, looked at Charlie, back to the sight of the kill, and said, "They're gonna need help rolling that beast off the hide," he grumbled and started back to where the women were working. He looked at Charlie. "It'll be up to you to tell the men what they're supposed to do!" he groaned.

———

ZEKE, Ted, Clara and Silas Hansen had tethered their horses near their wagons, anticipating an early hunt for meat before leaving, and now were recruited by Charlie and Eli to help round up the runaway horses and mules. They were joined by Noah Butler and Felix Carpenter from the trader's wagons and Eli directed the men to each take one of the teens as did he and Charlie, and they started south, backtracking the trail and following the tracks of the herd. They spotted a good bunch just south of their camp and Charlie had Noah Butler and Silas Hansen drive them back to the wagons, while the others continued south, following the tracks of the runaways. Charlie had dropped to the ground to look at the tracks, frowned, and looked up at Eli, "Uh, there's some other tracks, ridden horses, that have come from the hills, yonder"—nodding toward the buttes and mesas to the west about a half-mile— "the runaways had slowed, but the riders took off after 'em, less'n an hour ago." He rose, looked at Eli with one of those expressions that told Eli there was trouble ahead.

Eli asked, "The riders, natives or not?"

"Not." He swung back aboard his mount, pulled a

little closer to Eli and lowered his voice. "My guess is they were outlaws that had been layin' in wait for somebody, wagons or stages or sumpin', to take. Prob'ly thought our bunch was too big for 'em. Near as I can figger, there's only 'bout five or six of 'em."

Eli looked around at his riders, shook his head and explained, "Looks like there might be trouble up ahead. It appears there are some others that have taken off after the horses, and will prob'ly have 'em rounded up by the time we get there. Charlie thinks, and so do I, that whoever they are, they're up to no good. Outlaws that'll want to keep the horses and will fight for 'em." He looked at his group, knowing he had three young'uns, none of 'em more'n sixteen or so, and one experienced Indian fighter in Felix, and Charlie and himself. *Not much of an army,* he thought to himself. "Now, me'n Charlie are goin' after 'em, but you don't have to. You can return to the wagons and let folks know we'll be doin' what we can."

Zeke dropped his eyes to the ground, lifted them to Eli and said, "Is it alright if we come along? I'd like to help fetch them horses back to the wagons." He glanced to Ted and Clara, both of whom were nodding their heads in agreement, then he looked to Eli for an answer.

Eli grinned. "Do any of you have rifles?" All three snatched their rifles from the scabbards that hung beneath their stirrup fenders, and sat them on their legs, grinning. Eli chuckled, "It might get bad..." he cautioned, looking at each one and all three grinned, nodded, and Zeke said, "Let's go!"

Charlie led the way, often leaning to one side or the other to look at the tracks. He looked back to the others, pointed to the west, "Looks like the riders caught up with 'em, and they're headed o'er yonder way," pointing to the line of low buttes that stood out from the higher flat-top plateaus.

Eli nodded and came alongside Charlie. They sat, looking at the buttes, and Eli said, "I'm guessing they're just behind those buttes, waitin' for us to come after 'em." He leaned back, lifted his binoculars from the saddlebags, and took a long look. The buttes were on the west side of Sage Creek which was lined by stunted cottonwoods and alders that offered them cover from being seen too soon by the rustlers. But if there was someone atop the buttes watching for them, they would need binoculars to make them out, and Eli doubted if they had a pair, but he could not risk the young'uns.

As Eli continued to scan the terrain, trying to plan their next move, he heard a familiar voice. "We could cross over and come from the other side."

He dropped the binoculars from his eyes and looked to see Bluebird sitting her appaloosa beside him, shading her eye as she also looked toward the buttes. "What're you doin' here?" he asked, surprised at her sudden appearance.

She grinned. "I thought you could use the help of your scout."

Eli shook his head, grinning, glanced to see a laughing Charlie, and looked back at Bluebird. "I think you're right. They can't see us unless they have someone atop the buttes, but I could not see anyone up there." He motioned the others near. "I think a few of us will go across through the tall sage and the trees near the creek, go beyond that line of buttes, and come from the far side. I don't know exactly what the terrain is like there, but if most of you go with Charlie and go across and come at them from here, cuz they might have seen us and will be expecting us to come at 'em together, then the rest of us can come from their flank and give support."

"Who's goin' with you, Eli?" asked Zeke, hopefulness showing on his face and in his voice.

"Oh, I reckon Bluebird here, and maybe you Zeke. That way there'll be enough of the rest of you for them to think that's all of us."

Eli looked at Charlie and Felix, saw them nodding agreement, and the group started off together, bunching up so it would be hard for any observers to get a good count. Eli, Bluebird, and Zeke followed close behind until they were certain they were out of sight behind the tree-lined creek and they broke off from the others. Eli led the way, and they stayed behind the trees, moved upstream a little and at an opportune place with ample cover from the tree and the tall sage beyond the creek, they moved across the creek and stayed hunkered down in their saddles, moving across the sage covered flats until they came to the line of buttes.

Eli reined up, lifted his binoculars to see Charlie and the others spread out a little and moving closer to the buttes. He looked to Bluebird and Zeke. "Let's get movin'. We don't wanna be late to the party!" and bent to slip his Winchester from the scabbard. He had chosen to bring the Yellow Boy rifle instead of the Spencer, and still had his Colt revolving shotgun in the scabbard on the other side. They started at a fast walk down the narrow draw that split the flats between the low-rising buttes and the flanks of the higher plateaus.

Charlie and company came through a cut between two of the lowest buttes, and entered the wide draw, still following the tracks of the runaways. The wide draw had a low bench between the buttes and the mesas, offering a shallow gulley on either side. Charlie followed the tracks of the horses that kept to the gulley between the buttes and the bench, while Eli and company were on the far side of the bench.

Charlie saw a thin wispy line of smoke that rose from an apparent camp of the rustlers, near the back side of the tall butte. Between the smoke and Charlie, grazed the horses and mules, three men sat their saddles around the gathered animals, looking completely at ease, watching the horses and only one appeared to look at the incoming riders. Charlie reined up, stood in his stirrups to survey the area, noticed other men at the campfire, and guessed there would be six or seven of the men. He sat back in his saddle, spoke softly to his men. "There's three around the herd, three or four at the campfire, maybe another'n or two out of sight. Stretch out behind me, we'll move slow, and head around the herd toward the campfire." He looked at Felix. "There's one on that side"—nodding to the bench side— "of the herd, one behind 'em, and one on this side. The others are at the campfire 'tween the first one here and the second, yonder. We'll pass by this'n, but he's your responsibility. And if it starts, take him and the one on the far side. The rest of us will take them at the campfire."

"What about Eli?" asked Felix.

"We'll trust them to take the one at the back, and help us with those at the campfire and maybe that'n o'er yonder. They'll figger it out. Let's go," he stated, starting his mount forward. Clara followed close behind Charlie, her rifle across the bow of her saddle, followed by Ted and Felix.

Charlie nodded to the first man that sat on his mount, watching the herd and glanced indifferently to the visitors, but his grin told of trouble. The four filed past, Ted and Felix a little slower than Charlie and Clara.

Charlie had neared the campfire as those by the fire came to their feet, hands on holstered pistols, one man with a rifle cradled in his arms who stepped forward and greeted them with, "Howdy! You folks lost 'er sumpin'?" he asked, grinning.

Charlie reined up, Clara came alongside on his left, away from his right side where his pistol sat in the holster, and the rifle was laying across the pommel of his saddle. Charlie lifted his hand, pushed his hat back and said, "No, we ain't lost, just come after our horses. Wanted to thank you for roundin' 'em up fer us, but we'll take 'em from here." He reached down for his looped reins, grinning at the four men who looked at one another, watching the movements of their obvious leader, the talker.

The lead man chuckled, "Reckon you're mistaken, friend. These are all mustangs, an' we rounded 'em up for ourselves. Ain't nobody owned these hyar animals, no time, no where. These are ours, all of 'em, sure 'nuff. And since you're in our country, an' we got'chu outnumbered, our word is law!" he declared, starting to bring his rifle to bear, but was stayed when Clara cleared her throat to get his attention to see she had her rifle already pointed at his middle, and she was grinning. She said in a soft voice, "Just so you know, I can put a bullet through each of those two buttons and that tobacco tag 'fore you could jack a round in that there rifle." She smiled as she watched the big eyes of the man glance from her to Charlie and back.

"That's a woman!" he declared, shocked to see a woman here in the wilderness, and to see one with a rifle in her hand.

He made his statement of disbelief as if he expected Charlie to tell him different, but Charlie had grasped the grip of his Henry and was bringing it to bear when the man had looked to Clara. As he did, a rifle blasted from beyond the campfire and Charlie felt the bullet part his hair above his ear and he dropped the hammer on the man before him. The rifle of Clara also bucked and blasted, and the speaker was knocked back into the campfire, but he rolled from the flames and coals, smacking at the burning embers in his britches while blood flowed from the bullet hole in his chest. He crumpled to his knees, looked up with fear in his eyes at Clara, and fell face first into the fire. Both Charlie and Clara had jacked another round into their rifles and fired at another target behind the campfire and both took the same man, twisting him around on his heels before he fell to the ground, face first into the dust.

He was the man who had shot at Charlie, and now one more stood, staring at the two shooters and dropped his rifle, lifted his hands, and shouted, "No, don't shoot!"

Behind Charlie, two shots blasted almost simultaneously as Ted and Felix had turned to face the outrider for the herd, just as he had drawn his pistol and started to fire, but the bullets from the Henry and Spencer took him from the saddle and spooked the horses even more. Felix hollered to Ted, "Let's get them horses 'fore they run into them hills!" Both men dug heels and with rifles over their legs behind the pommels of their saddles, they took off to try to turn the horses. They heard firing from the far side of the herd, but they kept after the animals.

Eli and company had kept to the draw beyond the bench, but at the first rifle shot, he led the way as they charged over the top. He motioned to Zeke to take the outlaw rider beside the horses and he and Bluebird went after the drag rider and toward the camp. But the shooting from the camp continued and the horses jumped and pushed toward them, but Zeke had fired at the outrider just as he lifted his rifle to shoot at Zeke. Those shots pushed the horse herd to run north up the draw and Eli and Bluebird came in sight of the drag rider, who had his rifle in hand, looking toward the camp where most of the shooting was happening.

Eli slapped legs to Rusty and the big claybank lunged forward, driving toward the drag rider. Bluebird was close behind, but lying low on the neck of her appaloosa, Henry in hand and under the mane of the spotted horse. They came out of the dust looking like spectres of horror to the drag rider whose wide-eyed stare froze him in place until the big stallion Rusty slammed his chest into the side of the outlaws sorrel and knocked him to his side, pinning the outlaw who lost his rifle as he fell beneath the horse that was kicking and fighting to get back to his feet.

Eli pulled Rusty back, firmly told the man, "You move and you're a dead man!" Bluebird came alongside Eli, on the far side of the outlaw and said, "I think the shootings over," nodding toward the camp. Eli looked at the outlaw, "Git up, and start toward your camp!" The man slowly came to his feet, gave Eli an angry snarl, and said, "You're the one that's gonna be dead when Oscar gets you!"

"I think Oscar's done been got!" stated Eli, lifting the muzzle of his rifle to hustle the man along. He glanced back to Bluebird. "Watch the camp for any trouble."

She nodded, smiled, and lifted her rifle as she guided her appaloosa with her legs, all the while watching the activity at the camp. As they came near, they saw one man seated against a rock, his hands tied behind his back, three dead men, and Ted standing nearby, holding his rifle at the ready. He grinned up at Eli and Bluebird, glanced beyond them to see Zeke coming near, and said, "I think we got 'em. The others went after the horses."

Eli said, "Get mounted, and you and Zeke go help the others with the horses. We'll be along right quick." He looked at the walking outlaw and motioned with his rifle, "Get over there with that other'n." He watched Zeke and Ted leave to go help the others with the roundup and looked down at the two outlaws, he glanced to Bluebird, "Keep 'em covered."

She nodded, lifted her rifle to cover the outlaws as Eli stepped down.

He looked around at the gear of the others, found a piggin' string among the scattered gear and looked at the other outlaw. "Turn around and put your hands behind your back."

The man complied and was soon seated beside his fellow outlaw. Eli mounted up, looked at the two, "You could be just as dead as these others, hopefully you've learned somethin' here. You can get loose from those bonds sooner or later, and if you're lucky, you might find a horse or two wanderin' around hereabouts. If you're smart, you'll get outta this country, 'cuz next time, you won't be so lucky." He looked to Bluebird, "Let's go help the others."

CHAPTER 34

MOVING

They rode together, enjoying the lull after the storm of conflict, and were quiet as they started their scout of the trail in the early morning hours. The line of hills to the east lay in the shadows of early morning, the scars of deep rock canyons marring the face of the black-timbered hills. Behind the dark buttes, rose some snow-covered peaks that were tinted with the bright colors of the golden sunrise. The trail before them parted the sage and grassy flats, while to their left, the first rays of the rising sun bent over the horizon to color the rimrock of the long and broken plateau. It looked like it would be a clear day, only wisps of clouds remained after the stars snuffed out their lanterns, and the cool breeze of morning was refreshing on their faces.

Eli had grown contemplative, frowned in his quiet thoughts and looked at Bluebird who was smiling and enjoying the time together, and Eli asked, "You said your mother had a sister with a band near the Three Rivers, have you seen her recently?"

"She was with our band when my mother birthed my sister. She, my sister, is named after her, *Nanawu*, Little Striped Squirrel. But we have not seen her since my sister was born."

Eli frowned. "And your sister is fifteen summers?"

"Three hands, yes. What you call fifteen years old."

"Don't the Shoshone have a grand powwow where the different bands get together?"

"Yes, but not all come. The *Agaideka* and the *Tukkutikka* live in lands that are far from one another and it is not always easy to meet. We hear about other family members that do not come, but the word is not always right," she shrugged.

"But if she is no longer living, would you and Squirrel have a place with the *Agaideka*?"

"We are Shoshone, but since we do not have mates, the tribal council or chiefs could make us become the women of their chosen men. Many times it is with an older warrior that already has one or two wives. We would be their helpers."

"Could you take a man as your mate after that?"

"No, only if the man of the lodge dies."

Eli lapsed into a thoughtful silence, considering what he had learned. He knew he was fond of Bluebird and did not want to see her leave, but he was not sure enough of his feelings to consider her as a life mate or wife. But the thought of her becoming a third or fourth wife of some older warrior or chief, did not sit right in his mind. But as he faced that repugnant image, he realized he did not like the idea of her being any other man's first and only wife either. He took a deep breath, glanced to Bluebird and realized he had greater feelings for her than he wanted to admit. Then he had a troubling thought.

"If you were to be chosen for a wife, say by one of the warriors of the *Agaideka*, what about Squirrel?" asked Eli, frowning at the thought.

"Sometimes a warrior takes the sister as a second wife."

"But you could be made a wife of someone that already has two wives, and then Squirrel?"

"Could be given to the same or different warrior," She paused, looking at Eli, "Usually, those decisions are left with the father of the women. But since our father has gone, we have no one and will become a burden to the band of people we are with."

Eli shook his head, almost afraid to ask the next question that was swirling around in his mind, then blurted it out. "So, if you and I were to be joined, would I have to take Squirrel as my second wife?"

Bluebird smiled, laughter and happiness dancing in her eyes. She dropped her gaze, giggled a little and looked up at Eli. "No, unless you wanted to, but have you not seen what Squirrel has been doing?"

Eli frowned. "What has she been doing?"

"She and the young man Fredrick Hackworth are always together. He has told her he wants her for his wife."

"And what do his parents have to say?"

Bluebird smiled, shrugged and pursed her lips with a slight giggle and shook her head.

Eli shook his head. "That doesn't tell me anything. So..." he paused, looked at Bluebird, "You think they'll be joined or married?"

"Yes."

"When?"

"Anytime soon."

"So, among your people, when a man wants to marry a woman, doesn't he have to give the father a bride price, you know, horses or trade goods or something?"

"Yes. But she has no father, so that would come to me," smiled Bluebird.

"So..." began Eli, thinking things through. "If she marries first, then what happens when someone wants to take you for a mate? Does he have to pay you or your sister?"

"You would have to give me a good price for me!" she giggled.

Eli caught the 'you' she used and tried unsuccessfully to stifle a laugh, but they laughed together and the slight tension that had been between them melted in the puddle of laughter and Bluebird leaned toward Eli and he pulled her close, almost pulling her off her horse, but they enjoyed the moment.

The bottomland they traveled through had been formed by the river runoff from the hills to both east and west, but now it was little more than a trickle if anything, in a mostly dry riverbed. When they stopped for their nooning, the hills on the east showed themselves as a series of hogbacks with piñon covered west-facing slopes and to the west, marching to the north was a line of rimrock topped mesas that mimicked the hogbacks on the east. Together the ranges slowly narrowed the valley to funnel the travelers toward the green valley that carried the Yellowstone River, but they would not reach that river until dusk, and would cross it come daylight on the morrow.

Charlie had used several of the young men to ride with him on the scouting and hunting side trips and today Fredrick Hackworth had volunteered to side Charlie. As they left the trail behind the wagons, Charlie took a cut between the hogbacks on the east side of the trail, and the two hunters dropped into the greener valley that carried a live meandering stream that Charlie believed would merge with the Yellowstone River further north. He reined up at the edge of the greener grass, stood in his stirrups to look up and down the narrow vale that bent around a higher butte that slanted away from the creek and rose a couple hundred feet in a long slope that was mottled with piñon. He looked at his first-time companion and nodded to the willow lined stream.

"We should find some deer, maybe antelope or buffalo along this creek. We'll ride along this edge of the hills, get a better view of the bottom." He glanced to Fredrick, wondering, for he thought the young man had been a little fidgety or nervous for some reason.

Fredrick looked at Charlie, "Uh, can I ask you a question?"

"Sure Fred, anything. What's on your mind?" asked Charlie, nudging his mount to a walk to continue their hunt.

"Uh, you're Indian, aren't you?"

"Ummhmm, Pawnee," answered Charlie, frowning. "Why?"

"Well, me'n Squirrel, you know, Bluebird's sister, have been spendin' a lotta time together an' we're thinkin' 'bout gettin' married. She hasn't said, but ain't there some kinda thing the man has to do to get a girl to get married?"

Charlie grinned and chuckled. "What'chu mean, some way to ask or what?"

"Uh, like havin' to pay her father some stuff to get his word for her to marry?"

"Oh, I see. Well Fred, usually, yes. A man would have to pay a bride price whatever the father asks. Sometimes he wants horses, or other trade goods, like rifles and such. But..." he grinned and looked at the timorous young man, "Her father has crossed over, and her only family is Bluebird. So, I reckon you'd have to talk to her about what it'd take to let Squirrel marry you."

"You think it'd be a lot? I don't have much, but... but...I'd work hard and get what I could," he stammered, looking to Charlie, hopefully.

"I dunno. You'd hafta talk to Bluebird, but 'tween you'n me, that might depend on whatever she and Eli decide to do."

The young man frowned. "What's Eli got to do with it?"

Charlie grinned, "Oh, not much, I reckon. But I'm thinkin' he an' Bluebird might get together. I tell you what, I'll talk to Eli and Bluebird, see if I can get an idea what it might take, and I'll let you know, would that be alright?"

Fredrick smiled broadly, obviously relieved, and nodded as he answered, "Yeah, yeah, that'd be great! Thanks Charlie!"

"Don't go thankin' me too soon. But in the meantime, how 'bout'chu takin' a shot at that there mule deer yonder 'fore he sees us and spooks!" A big buck with velvet covered antler sprouts, had just lifted his head above the willows and looked about. He had probably heard the coming of the riders and was looking around.

Fredrick had dropped to the ground, took a shooting stance with legs spread, rifle to his shoulder and sighted on the deer and made a quick and accurate shot. The Henry bucked and blasted, spat smoke and lead, and the big buck blossomed red at the base of his neck. He sprung away to the far side of the creek, but fell to his chest, kicked once, and lay still.

"Good shot! Maybe you can give the hide to Squirrel, let her tan it for the two of you. You might learn somethin' there," observed Charlie, looking at the grinning and proud Fredrick.

CHAPTER 35

CHOICES

E li, Charlie, and Bluebird sat their mounts on the east bank of the Clark's Fork of the Yellowstone River, each contemplating the possibility of crossing and how it would best be done. Charlie offered, "Maybe one of us should cross o'er, see what it's like, you know, depth, current, such like."

"Charlie, that water's so clear you can see the bottom! And there's a sandbar yonder an' it looks like the deepest part is right out there!" declared Eli, leaning forward and pointing to the deeper blue/green waters this side of the sandbar. "And lookee yonder, them trout are jumpin' and havin' a good time. Maybe we should go fishin' 'fore crossin'!" He chuckled, glancing to Charlie and Bluebird.

Bluebird sat quietly, looking at the water and the far bank, then nudged her appaloosa to take to the water. The willing horse stepped into the water and started across. At the deepest point, about twenty yards from shore, the water chuckled under the appaloosa's belly without touching and Bluebird had lifted her feet until the appaloosa started across the gravelly sandbar and moved on across.

When on the far shore, she stepped down, let the mare shake off the excess and looked to the two sitting their mounts on the south bank and called out, "What're you waitin' on?"

Eli cupped his hands and hollered, "Alright you show off. We'll get the wagons started; you can catch us some fish for lunch!"

Bluebird smiled, waved and turned away as Eli and Charlie went to the waiting wagons. LaVerne Hackworth sat on his wagon, patiently holding the lines and watching the two men approach. It was his day to take the lead, and he was anxious to get across the river and get some miles behind them. The gold fever was showing in the man as he shaded his eyes, looking at the clear water river with the gravelly bottom, prime gold country.

As Eli approached, he sat back, looked at their guide and asked, "Ready to cross, is it?"

"It is. Looks to be an easy crossing, not too deep, 'bout fifty yards across and a good sandbar near the far bank. Just take it easy, keep to the trail and shouldn't have any problem."

"Good, good!" He grinned and slapped the reins to his four-up of mules and started to the crossing. Eli watched for a moment, saw Charlie working his way down the line of wagons, and Eli did the same. When he came to the wagon of Parson Spencer, he paused, pushed his hat back on his head and asked, "Say Parson, mind if I take a moment?"

"Of course not, Eli. What can I help you with?" he asked, keeping the lines of his team in his hand and leaning his elbows on his knees as he looked at Eli.

Eli chuckled, shook his head and stammered, "Uh, you do weddin's, don'tchu?"

"Sure 'nuff, but I thought you was already married?" asked the parson, frowning.

"No, no, I'm a widower. Lost my wife just after the war." He paused, frowning, and asked, "What made you think I was askin' for me?"

"Well, most men don't ask for others, it's usually for themselves. But I was kinda expectin' it, what with you'n Bluebird spendin' so much time together. Most everyone has been thinkin' you two'd end up together. I overheard a couple men wantin' to bet how long it'd take you to decide, and the women have been talkin' 'bout doin' up some sorta doin's for the occasion."

"So, how is it ever'body else knows more about my plans than my ownself?" asked an exasperated Eli, shaking his head and looking up and down the line of wagons.

The parson chuckled. "So, when you thinkin' of havin' this weddin'?"

"Wasn't really thinkin' of a shindig, just me'n her and you, you know, nothin' fancy. She ain't used to that kinda thing. With her people, they do get fixed up a mite, stand 'fore the shaman or chief, says a few words and puts their hands together and they run off to the marriage lodge."

"Ain't that about what you're expectin'?" asked the parson, grinning.

"I reckon, but you don't have any problem with me marryin' a native?"

"She seems to be a fine woman, Eli. I think you'll make a great couple. But..." He paused, looked around and lowered his voice, "How'd you feel if we had a double weddin'?

"A double weddin'? What'chu mean?"

"Well, that young Hackworth, Fredrick, was askin' the same questions just a bit ago, and rumor has it there might be another couple thinkin' 'bout gettin' hitched." The parson chuckled. "Must be somethin' in the air, course it is spring, ain't it?" he laughed, looking around at the beginning blossoms of wildflowers. "Just when were you thinkin' 'bout doin' this?"

"Well, we've only got about another day or two till we strike the Bozeman. That'll be 'bout as far as I go, so…" He shrugged.

"You're leavin' us?"

"That was the agreement. I was to guide you folks to the Bozeman Trail, and you'd take it from there. There's some good men on this train and it'll only be for a couple weeks till you get to Virginia City, and some folks are wantin' to go their own way 'fore that, so…"

The crossing of the Clark's Fork went well, the worst that happened was one of the Pedersen's boys, Reuben, jumped into the water for a swim, much to the chagrin of his mother, but his father warmed his britches after they crossed, and he probably would not be doing that again. They pushed on with the trail going due north and siding the Clark's Fork much of the way. They stopped for nooning about five miles north of the crossing and true to form, several of the gold hunters took the time to try panning for color, to no avail. But the habit had been formed, and any time they were near water, three or four or more of the men handed the reins to their women and jumped off the wagons to try a few pans.

The rimrock buttes and mesas on the west side of the long valley pushed in toward the winding river and the trail hugged the banks with the many cottonwoods, alders, and willows. After their nooning, they traveled about another eight to ten miles and rimrock buttes on the west receded, the rolling hills on the east diminished and the valley widened, and more green and other colors were showing. When there were ample trees for cover and grass for grazing, Eli signaled the wagons to circle up and make camp. It was about an hour short of dusk, and some were a bit surprised, but the gold hunters were glad for another chance at the promising waters that continued their northward flow. Charlie and Eli made camp in the trees on the bank of the river a little set apart from the wagons when Eli said, "You go ahead and finish things. I'm gonna go see if Bluebird got us any fish for supper!" he snickered, grinning at Charlie.

"You don't fool me. I saw you talkin' to the parson. I'm guessin' you and Bluebird are gonna be talkin' with him!"

"Ain't none o' your business, Charlie!" declared Eli, trying to be firm and staid, but failing as a grin split his face. He turned on his heel and walked away with Charlie chuckling as he left.

Eli went to the McCoy wagon, saw Bluebird and Squirrel helping Violet McCoy preparing something for their supper and saw several nice trout laid out on the makeshift table and being prepared for broiling. He grinned, asked, "I thought you were going to get some of those"—nodding to the fish— "for our supper?"

She smiled, laughed, "Those are for *our* supper. You and Charlie have been invited to take supper with the McCoy family and their daughters!" she said, nodding to Squirrel and touching her chest to indicate herself.

"Oh, I see how it is. Well, can I borrow the eldest daughter for a little bit? There's someone we need to talk to," he explained.

She smiled, nodded to a grinning Violet and went to

Eli's side. As they walked from the wagon, she asked, "And who is this someone we need to talk to?"

"Parson Spencer. He wants to talk to us before we get married," he stated without looking at her.

She stopped and grabbed at his arm. "What did you say?" she asked, showing a broad smile that danced in her eyes and she turned to face him.

"Oh, don't give me that. You heard me," he laughed and pulled her close. "Will you marry me Bluebird, and be my partner, friend and wife for the rest of our lives?"

She tiptoed, clasped her hands behind his head and pulled him down for a tender but passionate kiss. When they parted, she leaned back and with a broad smile looked up at him and said, "Yes!"

They walked hand-in-hand to the parson's wagon and were greeted by Zeke and Clara who were standing beside the wagon as the parson pulled some boxes from the wagon to use as benches. Zeke and Clara stood close, smiled and Clara asked, "So, you finally decided to do it, huh?" and giggled.

"Ummhmm, but what are you two doin'?" asked Eli.

Clara looked at Zeke and back to Eli. "Same thing and we're waiting for somebody else," she said, leaning to the side to see past Bluebird, expecting to see someone else. "But I guess they'll be along soon." As she spoke, she grinned and pointed to the third couple, Fredrick Hackworth and Little Striped Squirrel as they walked into the circle of friends.

"MY FATHER and mother told me about a White man, Henry Spalding and his wife, Eliza, who came into our land with others. They were going beyond our lands, but they stopped and told my people about your God and his son, Jesus. When we"—nodding to her sister— "were older, they told us what they knew and we did as they did, prayed and asked for forgiveness and to go to heaven with Jesus," explained Bluebird, much to the surprise of Eli. Although she had questioned him some, he never went into any greater discussion with the scriptures.

The parson smiled and nodded, and turned to Clara and asked, "And what about you, Clara?"

She smiled, dropped her eyes and began to explain. "When I was young, we went to the church in the village nearby. The pastor there spoke many times about accepting Christ as savior and one night my mother asked me if I had done that and I said, 'no, I don't know how.' She answered my questions and we prayed, and I accepted the gift of salvation that night."

The parson said, "Let me just do this. Let me explain why I've asked you about your faith. In I Corinthians 6:14 the Bible says, *Be ye not unequally yoked together with unbelievers: for what fellowship hath righteousness with unrighteousness*...and it continues with other examples. What God wants us to know is that it is best for both people in a marriage to know and believe the same. When He says *unequally yoked* that's from an example of a yoke of oxen or a team that pulls a wagon. Can you imagine a little burro harnessed together with a big mule or draft horse?" The listeners looked at one another, some shrugged, others grinned, but all looked back to the parson as he continued.

"See, it doesn't work very well to have such differences together. So, just so everyone understands, it's best for both to be together in their belief about God. So, to understand, the Bible tells us how we can be sure of Heaven as our home. First, we need to understand that we are all sinners, *Romans 3:23...*" He paused, looking at each one, and continued. "Now as I look at you, I think you all know that we're not perfect and we've had lives that included sin of some kind, am I right?" They looked at the parson, one another, and all agreed.

"Then we also need to know that because we're sinners, there is a penalty, and that penalty is death and hell forever, *Romans 6:23* but God didn't want us to go to Hell, so he made a way to avoid that, and He sent his son to pay the penalty for us. He sent Jesus to the cross to die for all of us, *Romans 5:8,* and when he did that, he paid for our sins and paid for the gift He has for us, which is the gift of eternal life, to live in Heaven with Him forever. *Romans 6:23.* Now, that's just like any gift, for it to be ours, we have to accept it and we do that through prayer, *Romans 10:9-13.* So, if you don't know for sure, but you want to be sure, here's what we'll do. I'm going to pray, and if you want to receive that gift of eternal life, or want to make sure, you just repeat that part of the prayer I tell you." He looked around at each one, then bowed his head and began to pray.

As he started to pray and paused, glanced up at the others and continued with, "Now, if you want to make sure of Heaven, then repeat after me, and don't do it unless you really mean it." He paused again, then continued. "Dear God, I want to trust you today to take me to Heaven when I die. Forgive me of my sins, and give me the gift of eternal life paid for by Jesus on the cross. Thank you God, and help me to be the best Christian I can, in Jesus's name, Amen."

The parson smiled as he looked up and around at each one. He wasn't sure, but it sounded like just about everyone prayed the prayer. But he wanted to be certain, so he added, "So, if you prayed that prayer, and you meant it with all your heart, then take my hand," and extended his hand and Squirrel was the first to grab his hand, followed by Fred, Zeke, and Bluebird.

"Wonderful!" declared the parson, and added, "Now, let's talk about tomorrow," and began sharing about how the service would go since it was Sunday and they would have a worship service for everyone first, followed by the wedding service.

Everyone was happy, excited, and eagerly anticipating the following day. As they left the parson's wagon, Eli and Bluebird walked with Fred and Squirrel to return to the McCoy wagon, saying little, but thinking about many things, the couples holding hands as they walked.

CHAPTER 36

COMMITTED

The four men stood beside their horses as Eli began to explain, "That's Rock Creek in the bottom there. The trail comes across the flats and crosses there at the cut in the trees. You can see the trail on the far side. It bears west and into those hills and your first night camp will probably be overlookin' the Yellowstone River. After that, the trail continues west followin' the river for 'bout a week, then you'll come to the town of Bozeman. The last time I saw that town it wasn't much, but it did have a general store that was pretty well stocked. You might want to spend a day there for everyone to rest up and such." He looked at the men who were looking into the distance and at the surrounding terrain, listening intently.

The two captains, Nolan Thorne and Mark Ryan stood beside one another, the third man, Arne Pedersen, was the big lumberjack with four youngsters, two of the strapping young men that had repeatedly been a help to others and never a problem. The captains had asked Arne to join them and as he stood close, he dwarfed the other two, standing most of a head above them with a chest that rivaled that of most horses. His tawny mane and beard bounced when he laughed, and his deep voice seemed to stir the countryside.

He looked at Eli. "Kinda wisht you was comin' wit' us, but I'm shore we can do it alright."

"Well, it's only a couple weeks further. One week to Bozeman, and a short week south to Virginia City. And the way it's been goin', several of these wagons will be droppin' off when they find promising land or..." He shrugged, grinning. Eli glanced at the other men, and continued, "Now, after you leave Bozeman, you'll continue west, cross the Gallatin River, and about a day later, you'll cross the Madison, then you'll head south two or three days to Virginia City."

"The way you tell it, it sounds easy enough. So, we're thinkin' maybe two weeks?" asked Nolan, glancing from Eli to Mark and Arne and back.

'Bout that, as you know, there can always be unexpected delays, but the trail from here on has been traveled much more than what we've come over so it should be considerably easier. There will be a stretch this side of the town of Bozeman where the trail divides, and it's up to you which one you take. The north one crosses the Yellowstone, goes over Bozeman Pass, and down into Bozeman. The other'n stays south of the river and straight into the town."

"Which would you take?" asked Mark Ryan.

"Couldn't say, never been over 'em, so I suggest you have someone scout it out and then decide," answered Eli, turning to mount up to return to the camp. The others followed and rode quietly, pondering what lay before them, as did Eli, but he was thinking of his life with Bluebird. They had talked a little about what they would do, but had yet to decide. He thought they would just go to the mountains, maybe southwest to the Absaroka Mountains, and just take some time for themselves and talk things over before making any life-changing decisions.

———

WHEN THE MEN rode back into the camp, it was a beehive of activity with everyone making ready for the church service and the word had spread about a wedding and the women were tittering and fixing and cooking and planning while the men did their bidding by sitting up benches, chairs, anything to make do for church pews, and a raised platform for the parson and the weddings. Something so simple had become a major production and Eli shook his head as the men separated and went to their wagons.

Eli rode into the small clearing in the cottonwoods where he and Charlie had made their camp and was greeted by a grinning Charlie, "So, you're gettin' married today!" he chuckled. Eli grinned, stepped down, and began stripping the gear from Rusty. He had no sooner given Rusty a rubdown when Violet McCoy called out, "Hello the camp! May I come in?"

Charlie answered, "C'mon in and welcome!"

Violet looked from Charlie to Eli and extended a package toward Eli with, "This is from Bluebird. She says you are to wear it this morning. She would have brought it to you, but…" She shrugged, grinning, and Eli knew the women were up to something because it wasn't every day that sisters get married.

Eli accepted the package. "Thank you, Mrs. McCoy.

Sorry to be putting you through all this trouble, that wasn't what I expected."

She laughed, covering her mouth as she did and looking a bit coy as she grinned at Eli, "Well, you know us women. But it will be very nice." She turned away, smiled, waved over her shoulder and walked back to the circle of activity at the wagons.

Eli opened the parcel and was surprised to find a man's tunic of white tanned buckskin and intricate beading and fringe. He held it up to see and was amazed at the elaborate beading that crossed the chest and back, meeting at the shoulders. Long fringe hung from the sleeves and shirt tail with beading going down the sleeves. The beadwork was predominantly blue with red and yellow accents, the pattern showed diamond shapes of contrasting colors and what appeared to be lances formed of beads. It was a heavy garment, but beautiful.

He looked at Charlie who stood spellbound as they looked at the garment and said, "It's a groom's shirt," and held it to his chest. "Reckon I better take a dip and wash off, shave and such, 'fore I put this on."

"Better git it done, the parson's gonna start church real soon!" offered Charlie.

———

ELI, clean shaven, hair combed and wearing his new tunic, walked beside Charlie as they entered the circle of wagons to join everyone for the church service. The people were standing, and the parson just finished a short prayer, and they began singing,

> *Shall We Gather at the River.*
> *Shall we gather at the river?*

> *Where bright angel feet have trod*
> *With its crystal tide forever,*
> *flowing by the throne of God.*
> *Yes we'll gather at the river,*
> *the beautiful, beautiful river*
> *Gather with the saints at the river*
> *that flows by the throne of God.*

Several had noticed Charlie and Eli arriving, and Eli's shirt immediately caught their attention as shown by several that looked, turned to tell someone nearby, and they looked. But Eli and Charlie stood at the rear and listened as the parson began his sermon.

"This mornin' I want to talk about the purpose of our life and my text is from I Corinthians 6:20 *For ye are bought with a price: therefore glorify God in your body, and in your spirit, which are God's.*" He enthusiastically spoke about how the purpose of our life is to glorify God. He explained it with the idea of shining a light on the subject or focusing our attention on one thing so that others would see that one thing more clearly, and that one thing should be God.

The parson spoke on his subject for about fifteen minutes, and closed with a prayer and an invitation, "Now folks, you cain't glorify anything if you don't know what it is. So if you're not sure about who and what God is, and if you can't say that He is your Savior and you know you have eternal life and will be in Heaven with him, then you need to see me after this is o'er and let me show you how you can know for sure!" With that, he explained, "Now, let's all stand, maybe sing another verse while folks get ready for the next part of our service this morning."

ELI AND FRED and Zeke had been hustled off away from the others until their preparations were finished. When Charlie came for the men, he pointed them to the aisle that had been formed by the people pushing benches back and all standing and waiting. Opposite the men were the three brides, with Bluebird standing a little closer, smiling and dropping her eyes coyly. She had on a beautiful white tanned dress that had extensive beadwork in the same style, color and fashion as that on Eli's tunic only much more. The beadwork crossed her chest and shoulders, and draped down the front of her dress with a fringe of beads at each side. The beads also extended down the arms and accented the long fringe that hung to her knees. The fringe ended with dyed tufts of rabbit fur that matched the colors of the beadwork. But as beautiful as the craftsmanship of the attire, Eli's attention was focused on the woman before him. Her hair was parted, and long braids that were accented with tufts of fur and beaded flowers that hung to her waist. A large pom of white fur with a blossom of red and green beads sat jauntily above her left ear, and a beaded headband graced her head. She smiled at her man, extended her hands, and they came together, turning to walk down the aisle.

They were followed by Zeke and Clara, both dressed in their finest with Clara adorned with a special hairstyle done up by her mother and hanging loosely over her shoulders. Her broad smile told of her happiness. They were followed by Squirrel and Fred, who were attired similar to Bluebird and Eli, only not quite as detailed and colorful, but beautiful, nevertheless.

———

FOR SUCH AN UNUSUAL wedding with three couples, the parson made it short and sweet, having each one repeat the usual wedding vows, and seal those vows with a kiss, and a shout of joy from the crowd. Everyone stood, marched along the 'receiving line' of three couples and gave their best wishes and hurried to the layout of a festive meal, prepared by all the ladies who had worked since last night and tended the cooking through the night. The men had done their part by preparing separate and private campsites with campfires and lean-tos for each couple complete with fresh bedding given by the people of the wagons as their collective gifts.

After the meal, they had an old-fashioned hoe-down with fiddles, squeezeboxes, guitars, and even a flute that magically appeared from the gear that had been carried thus far. It was a joyous celebration for everyone. Most of the journey was behind them and all were looking to the future, especially the newlyweds, and with dreams galore and promises made, it was a tired group that turned in for the night.

———

"WELL CHARLIE, reckon this is where we part comp'ny!" declared Eli, standing beside his saddled mount and packhorse. Charlie had traded Catlin out of one of their spare horses to have a pack horse of his own, and he had packed up his gear and was also ready to leave. He looked at his friend, grinning, and the two stepped close and gave one another a bear hug. When they stepped back, Charlie said, "Now you know my missus, Meaghan, after she births our young'un is gonna be 'spectin' you and your new wife to come visitin' don'tchu?"

"Yeah, I reckon. And we'll be doin' that too, just don't know when or how soon. We're goin' to the mountains" —he pointed to the southwest— "the Absarokas, have some time together and look things o'er before decidin' where we want to settle. Might just wander the mountains the rest of our lives, who knows?" He chuckled. "But we'll come see you an' your'n," he drawled, giving a twang that was unnatural for him, but he grinned in the doing of it, which elicited a grin from his friend.

"Wal, we'll be lookin' fer you and keep a light out fer you!" answered Charlie.

They had said their goodbyes to the people of the wagon train as they pulled out at first light. Squirrel and Fred were going to go with his folks, as were Clara and Zeke, leaving the two friends on their own. Charlie stepped into his stirrup, swung aboard and grinned at his friend, "Watch your topknot!"

"You too!" answered Eli as Bluebird came beside him, slipping her arm around his waist. They watched Charlie leave and Eli turned to his bride, gave her a lingering kiss and said, "Well, woman, reckon we need to get a move on. We wanna be in the mountains 'fore dark!"

She laughed and answered, "Whatever you say, husband," and giggled as she swung aboard her appaloosa. She had received a blue roan mare as a bride price from Fred and it was packed with the rest of Bluebird's belongings.

They rode across the green valley with the morning sun stretching the shadows, and as the shadows shortened, the sun warmed their shoulders. They rode side by side, often reaching out to touch one another and enjoying the beauty of God's creation. There were no set plans, no predetermined directions, other than the mountains, just a time of enjoying one another, sharing with one another, and becoming one together.

Eli looked to the cloudless blue sky and said, "Thank you, God!"

A Look At: The Trail to Redemption

Plainsman Western Series Book One

A BRAND-NEW CLASSIC WESTERN SERIES FROM BEST-SELLING AUTHOR B.N. RUNDELL.

Every time he squeezed the trigger, somebody died. He thought it was just the way of the war, but after taking a couple bullets and being mustered out, it continued. When he stood over the ashes of his family's farm and stared at their graves, the same bile rose in his throat, and he knew somebody was going to have to pay… and pay with their blood.

This was to be the beginning of a blood hunt that would take Reuben Grundy across four states, pit him against renegade outlaws posing as the Home Guard for the north, the Bushwhackers of Captain Quantrill and the men in butternut and grey, as well as the mighty Pawnee of the plains. His father had taught young Reuben to never look for others to do what needs to be done, even if it means putting his life on the line. And Reuben would do just that, with his training as one of Berdan's Sharpshooters at the outset of the war between the states, and his own time beside his father in the woods, Reuben was destined to become one of the most feared hunters of the plains.

Whether it was for man or beast, when his sights settled on the target, death was sure to follow.

AVAILABLE NOW

ABOUT THE AUTHOR

Born and raised in Colorado into a family of ranchers and cowboys, B.N. Rundell is the youngest of seven sons. Juggling bull riding, skiing, and high school, graduation was a launching pad for a hitch in the Army Paratroopers. After the army, he finished his college education in Springfield, MO, and together with his wife and growing family, entered the ministry as a Baptist preacher.

Together, B.N. and Dawn raised four girls that are now married and have made them proud grandparents. With many years as a successful pastor and educator, he retired from the ministry and followed in the footsteps of his entrepreneurial father and started a successful insurance agency, which is now in the hands of his trusted nephew.

He has also been a successful audiobook narrator and has recorded many books for several award-winning authors. Now realizing his life-long dream, B.N. has turned his efforts to writing a variety of books—from children's picture books and young adult adventure books, to the historical fiction and western genres, which are his first loves.